THE ILLUSTRIOUS CORPSE

THE ILLUSTRIOUS CORPSE

TIFFANY THAYER

CUTTING EDGE

ISBN-13: 978-1-962896-78-8

Published by
Cutting Edge Books
PO Box 8212
Calabasas, CA 91372
www.cuttingedgebooks.com

TO THEDA

*who prefers them
bloody, but takes
them all just as
they come*

CONTENTS

CHAPTER ONE

1
THAT FUNNY FEELING

THE ADULT WAIF sucked air noisily through his nose; he had a cold. His weight shifted from this foot to that.

"I seem to know where a man's been killed," he said, and his eyes wavered from those of the police lieutenant.

"Yeah? Well, who are you?"

"I"—sniff—sniff—"I don't exactly know." He gave a silly laugh, and again his eyes went roving toward the ceiling of the precinct station.

"Whadaya mean y'don't know?"

The officer frowned.

After all, he didn't have to be here telling them. It was out of the goodness of his heart he had come. He just wanted to do the right thing. There was no use growling at him like that.

"Oh, never mind." He turned to leave. Let them work out their own problems. He wasn't a cop. It was none of his business.

"Whadaya mean, 'never mind'? What the devil is this? What's your name?" The lieutenant came up out of his chair and stood with his frown deepening as he glowered.

"Now, there's no use yelling at me. I only thought maybe you'd like to know how I felt. It's a very funny feeling, and it just seems as if somebody'd been killed there."

"Somebody'd been killed *where?*"

"In the men's wash room on Forty-fifth Street, but I guess there's nothin' to it. I guess it's just a crazy idea. I won't bother you any more."

"Now, wait a minute."

The man was altogether too anxious to leave.

"Don't be in such a hurry. Sit down."

Evidently, the fellow was sorry he had started this.

"Oh, never mind. Never mind. I guess it's just a notion."

"Whereabouts on Forty-fifth Street?" the lieutenant asked with a crude attempt to make his tone chatty.

"Oh, well—now, I don't know the number exactly. It's a place about the middle of the block."

The lieutenant placed a chair carefully beside his desk and motioned the nondescript into it.

"Have a smoke," he said and pushed a package of cigarettes within reach. The hand that stretched toward them trembled and Lieutenant Miller squinted one suspicious eye at the dirty nails. Who could tell? This bird was full of coke. A bum! He couldn't look you in the eye. Conscience——

"Thanks." The fellow sat down and brushed at the soup-strewn front of his coat.

Somewhat expansively, when his cigarette was lighted, he said: "I don't suppose there's anything in it, lieutenant. But every time I go in that little room I get the idea that a man's been killed there. I can almost see him on the floor with a big gash on the back of his neck. It's got so bad I don't go there any more. And I thought I'd tell the police how I felt. Maybe you know about somebody bein' killed there."

The lieutenant nodded his head non-committally. "Well, near there maybe. What's your name?"

"I don't know. You see, my memory's gone. I used to know who I was, but—I—I guess I don't know any more."

"Memory's gone, eh? Where do you live?"

"Well, I've been living uptown, now. Up on Eighty-fourth Street. Nice room—nice lady."

Lieutenant Miller took up a pencil. "What number on Eighty-fourth Street?"

"Now, look here. I don't want any trouble. I don't want to be mixed up with any police trouble. And I don't want any police comin' out there to my room. I offered to tell you about my funny feelin'. You didn't catch me. I ain't done nothin' to be caught for. I just came in here to help you. I'm not lookin' for trouble."

"Who said anything about trouble? We ain't gonna make you no trouble, Mr.——What did you say your name was?"

"I didn't say. I forgot my name."

"Well, ain't that a little peculiar? How come you to forget your name?"

"I ain't been well."

" 'At's too bad. Y'ought to let the hop alone an' you'd be well enough." The officer rose. "Come in here!"

"No, I won't. I'll just let you solve your own mysteries. I ain't got nothin' to do with it, anyway."

"Come in here!"

Lieutenant Miller yanked the bewildered citizen into a smaller room. Quickly, his hands went through the fellow's pockets. He found thirty cents, a soiled handkerchief, and a corner torn from the want-ad section of a morning paper.

"You lookin' for a job?"

"Yes, sir."

"Set down."

The citizen complied.

"Bill!"

An officer dropped his magazine and answered.

"Book this guy for vagrancy. I'm goin' across the hall."

Detective headquarters was across the hall. Lieutenant Miller leaned his shiny elbows on the desk of the chief. "A vag jus' wandered in, coked to the ears. He dreamed about a murder in a men's room on Forty-fifth Street. Want to see him?"

"That guy Daniels was croaked in a wash room on Forty-fifth, and dragged down four flights of steps."

"This may be a lead."

"It's Brubacher's case. Hey, Brubacher, Miller's got a Daniels lead for you."

Brubacher slowly unfolded more than six feet of detective and yawned at the two men. "Daniels?"

"Yeah, he's got 'im across the hall."

"Yizzah." The giant followed the lieutenant into the hall. "I heard o' these 'leads' before. Nothin' ever comes of 'em."

"He's full o' hop."

"The chief? Yeah. He was a good detective when Grant took Richmond."

"Not him. This guy."

"Oh, I thought you meant the boss."

"Oh, boy! That's a good one."

The tipster was smiling when Miller and Brubacher entered. "This policeman has given me a name!" he beamed. "A name I can remember—Richard Roe. Gee!" He turned and shook the wearied hand of the cop. "Thanks again. Ain't that great? Richard Roe. Wait till I tell Sybil."

"Who's Sybil?" asked the suspicious lieutenant quickly.

"Oh, she's a girl where I live. She got me these clothes."

"Yeah? Ain't they yours?"

"No. I guess I lost mine. But she's an awful good kid."

Miller turned to Brubacher. "Get it? He claims he's lost his memory. Don't know who he is. And he has dreams about a guy bein' killed. Now he says he's lost 'is clothes."

Richard Roe, fresh from the baptismal font of the precinct police station, looked up at Brubacher. "Are you a detective?"

"Guilty."

He turned to Miller and asked: "Is he?"

"He jus' told you he was."

"I didn't hear him."

Apparently, this was comic. The three officers laughed.

"Where do you have these dreams, Roe?"

"Always in this wash room on Forty-fifth Street."

"Yeah? What number?"

"I don't know the number, but I can take you there."

"Aw right. Let's go."

"I got him booked for vagrancy—just to hold 'im. So don't let 'im get away."

"Don't worry! This guy looks phony to me. I'll see what's bitin' him."

Brubacher and Richard Roe walked down the street together. "Don't try to make a bust for it, Roe, 'cause I'll drill you sure as anything."

Roe was genuinely surprised. "Oh, I don't want to get away. I'm glad to do this for you. Has there ever been a murder reported in that room?"

"What are you tryin' to do, kid me?"

"No, I'm not kidding. Has there?"

"Don't you read the papers?"

They waited at a corner for a stream of autos to pass.

"Well, I haven't been reading them lately. I've tried, but they don't seem to mean nothin'. As soon as I'm through with 'em, it's all gone and I don't know a thing I've read."

"On the level?"

"I suppose it's hard for you to understand, but that's the way it gets me. I can remember where I live, now, and I can remember the other people there, but, unless they write it down, I can't get all the things they tell me."

"How far is this joint?"

"Just another block, and around the corner."

Brubacher was measuring his man. He trusted no one. He doubted even deathbed confessions. A plea of "guilty" was only a legal dodge to Brubacher. All men were liars—thrice liars when accused of crime.

They passed the fire exit of the Bond Building on Forty-fifth Street where a body had been found a month before. Richard Roe looked at the doorway and paused, turning to Brubacher.

"Well," the detective growled. "What's the trouble?"

"I feel very funny about that doorway. I never noticed *that* before."

Thus the calmness of an autumn day was disturbed for the police department. Thus was started the most peculiar chain of circumstances ever recorded in criminal annals. All was peace and tranquillity until this nameless man with a head cold blundered into the arms of the law and started seemingly endless investigations. But for the mental disturbance of Richard Roe, and his attempt to give the police a helping hand, a half dozen crimes would have remained undetected, and as many miscreants unpunished.

2
GRUESOME

OCTOBER 3rd was windy, and the force of the wind did not abate at sunset. About nine in the evening, two young men passed the Bond Building on Forty-fifth Street. As one of them stepped into a doorway out of the wind to light a cigarette, his foot encountered a soft object. He struck a match and discovered a lifeless body. Together they carried it across the street to an undertaking parlor and rang the night bell for admittance.

A sallow, nervous youth in shirt sleeves was finally aroused from the depths of the place, and he helped them deposit their burden on a table in the rear of the establishment.

"You fellows should of called a cop. You hadn't ought to bring 'im in here."

"Can't *you* call a cop?"

"Sure, but it ain't right. It's a medical examiner's job, and the body ought to be left right where it's found."

"Well, we don't want to be mixed up in it. Called to court and all."

"Like jury duty."

"Yeah."

"You don't expect us to carry it back, do you?"

"Well, you'll have to wait here till the wagon comes. I ain't got no right to let you go."

"Wait, hell!"

"Why should we wait?"

"Well, how'd I know you didn't bump this guy off yourselves?" The youngster was moving toward the phone.

"Don't you call the police for five minutes, young fellow. Good night."

"Hey, wait a minute. Where'd you say you found this guy?"

"In the freight door of the Bond Building, right across the street. So long."

"So long, and to hell with you! You got me in a fine mess."

The two young men continued their way down the street.

"I always thought an undertaking parlor *was* kind of a police station."

"Me, too. Dead people, and all."

"I don't want to testify and all that."

"Me neither."

"Fresh kid. Tryin' to keep us there."

"Yeah. You think we ought to tell a cop?"

"I donno. He'll call 'im, I guess."

"We wouldn't have to say we found 'im. Just tell 'im the undertaker wants to see 'im."

"Aw right. This guy?"

"Yeah, you tell 'im?"

"Why don't you?"

"I ain't scared."

While his friend waited, the shorter of the two approached the patrolman on an opposite corner.

"The undertaker sent me to get you, officer. Somebody's been killed, and they got 'im there."

"How'd they get killed?"

"I donno. He just asked me to get a policeman."

The officer started rapidly for the undertaker's. The young man rejoined his companion, and they left the vicinity as quickly as they could.

3
CAB CHASE

A VERY frightened boy answered the clatter of the policeman's nightstick on the door.

"What's the trouble?" asked the officer, pushing past the trembling assistant.

"Two—t-t-two fellows just brought a man in here and left him. I t-t-t-told 'em they should of got you and left him where they found 'im."

"Where'd they find 'im?"

"Across the street."

"Who is he?"

"I donno."

"Who brought 'im in?"

"Two fellows."

"I on'y saw one fellow. You got 'im in back?"

"Yeah."

"Keep 'im. I'm gonna see if those guys are still around."

Pell-mell, he dashed to the street and back to the corner. Two men lounged in a shadow. Seeing the police box on the corner, the officer remembered routine and unlocked it. Before the desk answered, the two men started to move away. Hurriedly, he spat the necessary facts into the telephone, and, slamming the box, started in pursuit. The two men had entered a cab, and, as the traffic lights changed, sped away uptown. The officer mounted the running board of a passing car.

"Follow that cab! Step on it!"

CHAPTER TWO

1
TOM,—NOT THE PIPER'S SON

TOM, the embalmer's apprentice, was confronted with a novel situation. In the first place, he had made some plans of his own for that evening—plans which did not include the sudden intrusion of strange bodies and the law. For many days, he had been waiting for his opportunity. This night had started auspiciously by the boss embalmer leaving him early alone. His small spirit had expanded under the vicarious responsibility.

Tom had not noted the agitation of his superior as he took his leave. He was himself too excited at the imminence of his big chance. He only wanted to be alone. In the back room lay the body of an illustrious lawyer, killed the day before in an auto accident. He would be buried the next day from the Chandler chapel, with pomp and panoply suitable to so eminent a personage.

Young Chandler himself was dashing back to town from Aiken, just because the funeral was so important. He would be down early—Tom knew his ways—fussing around, handling everything, moving the palms, twisting the satin and velvet hangings, arranging and rearranging the floral tributes. Funny, but he had no feeling for the undertaking business. He only carried on because his father who founded the organization had wanted him to. He'd cut a pretty figure trying to embalm a body himself. What a pill! But outside of business, he was all right. Good-looking devil!

Then, while the boy's head swam with his own future plans, these two fools were finding the body of this poor fellow and bringing it to him. He had helped them put it on a table next to the body of the lawyer. He had bluffed about calling the police and had seen them leave with a feeling of immense relief. He had relocked the front door and gone back to look at the new arrival. His movements were nervous. He snatched at the buttons. What should he do about this? He stripped the body with practiced hands, scarcely aware of what he was doing. What had he done? Should he be undressing this unidentified body? Could he be held? Why had he not refused to let the men bring it in?

Then the cop had not entered the back room—had flown in pursuit of the two fellows. He scurried furtively to the draped doorway. The policeman had gone. No one was passing. This was his chance, but he would have to hurry.

2
—TWO OTHER GUYS

THE overly zealous policeman continued to follow the taxi. Finally it stopped, and the two men alighted. He accosted them and knew his mistake at a glance. He had never seen either of them before. The man who had spoken to him was not there. They denied, in shocked surprise, any knowl<edge of a dead man. The policeman had to admit that this was probably true. He could not arrest them for riding in a taxicab. He hurried back toward his own beat. Two blocks from Chandler's Undertaking Parlor, No. 4, fire apparatus was arriving. Here was new duty. What the devil should he do? He ran toward the smoking store front.

Twenty minutes later, his lieutenant arrived at the scene of the fire. The patrolman saluted.

"There's a body been found, lieutenant. It's in Chandler's morgue. I didn't get a look at it. I was chasing the men who found it."

"Dead?"

"Yes, sir. Found in a doorway."

"In Chandler's?"

"Yes, sir."

"You call the wagon?"

"Yes, sir."

"That's all right. He won't go 'way till the wagon comes."

"It's kind of a funny case."

"You better stay here. If you reported, the medical examiner'll take care o' the body."

"Yes, sir."

3
EXIT BODY

WHILE fire ravaged the basement of a furrier's two blocks away, the dead wagon arrived at Chandler's Undertaking Parlor. Two uniformed men with a stretcher between them found the front door unlocked. A dim light in the reception room revealed nothing but massive, unoccupied furniture. They proceeded through the familiar passage to the back room.

"Hello, Chandler!"

There was no response.

"Hey, Chandler, you got callers!"

"Where the devil is everybody?"

The back room was thoroughly lighted.

"Gosh, they didn't do a thing to that guy's face, did they?"

Examination of the premises revealed no one in attendance.

"Well, we can't wait all night. Let's take 'im."

"There ought to be somebody around."

"Aw right. Let's wait. I ain't got nothin' to do."

But waiting availed nothing. The chauffeur finally came back to see what detained the doctors.

"There ain't nobody here."

"What of it! Let's take this bird and beat it!"

"Where's 'is clothes?"

"There."

So the boys rolled the body from the table to their stretcher. They covered him with a sheet, and pushed their way through a gathering crowd to their dismal conveyance.

"Shall I shut this door?"

"Sure."

"It'll lock."

"Let 'er lock! What the hell!"

The door of Chandler's clicked shut, and the wagon drove to the morgue.

That door was not opened again until Joe Chandler, owner of the chain of undertaking parlors, unlocked it himself the next morning at eight o'clock.

4
COLD PRINT

An item in the morning newspapers, October 4th, ran as follows:

HOLDUP MEN MURDER
ON FORTY-FIFTH STREET

———

Frank Daniels, Trenton Merchant
Found Dead in Street

———

The body of Frank Daniels, wealthy hardware merchant of Trenton, New Jersey, his face and head horribly mangled, was found last evening by two men, who fled without giving their names. Robbery was the motive of the gruesome crime, according to the police. Money and valuables had been stripped from the body, and only letters and cards in the pockets served as identification.

A search has been instituted for Thomas Freeman, nineteen, an undertaker's assistant, who is mysteriously missing.

All efforts to communicate with Mrs. Daniels in Trenton have been fruitless. The Trenton officials are attempting to ascertain her whereabouts.

CHAPTER THREE

1
THE CHAIN STORE UNDERTAKER

BRUBACHER and Pearlman were detailed to solve the murder of Frank Daniels. Receipts, letters and cards of membership in various lodges in the pockets of a decent business suit established the man's identity. "Frank Daniels, hardware merchant, Trenton, New Jersey." Telegrams were dispatched. The Trenton police were enormously excited. The hardware store was under the management of an assistant. Mrs. Frank Daniels had disappeared.

Pearlman went over to Trenton to help the boys out.

Brubacher handled the other end. He went to Chandler's.

"I'm Brubacher, from detective headquarters."

Joe Chandler was pacing the thickly carpeted floor. "How do you do?"

"Is the fellow here who took in that body las' night?"

"What body?" The young millionaire stiffened, every tense muscle alert to defend himself.

"That guy they found."

"I don't know anything about it."

"Are you Chandler?"

"Yes."

"Was you here las' night?"

"I was on a train until two this morning."

"Oh, yeah?" Brubacher, sensing an alibi, was openly skeptical. "A train, eh?"

"Yes, a train. I came here for the Macnaughton funeral."

"Macnaughton, eh?"

"Yes, Macnaughton."

"H'm! Where's the guy that was here las' night?"

"That's what I should very much like to know."

"Whadaya mean?"

"I mean that two of my employees are missing with eight thousand dollars of my money."

"The hell they are!"

Brubacher stared at the young man with characteristic unbelief. "Did you report it?"

"No."

"Well, you better. My God! Eight thousand bucks!"

"I don't know. I'm waiting. The—the night man may be able to explain it when he comes on duty to-night."

"Yeah, if he comes. You said he was missin'."

"I haven't been able to get him by phone. That really doesn't mean anything."

"What time is he due?"

"At five."

"I'll be here. I want to ask him some questions."

"So do I. What body was brought here?"

Brubacher squinted at the young mortician.

"Don't you know nothin' about it?"

"I do not. I came here at eight this morning, and I haven't seen either of my men since. I'm going to discharge them both when I do see them."

"Yeah! What for? The eight thousand?"

"Oh, that will turn up. Charley has that with him for safe-keeping. But what makes me sore is leaving me alone here to-day with this big funeral on my hands."

"Macnaughton?"

"Yes. What if I had decided not to come back? Good God, what a mess!" Again the young man began pacing the floor, his hands clenched behind him.

Brubacher sagely made a mental record that Joseph Chandler had been robbed of eight thousand dollars, and, for some reason of his own, wished to take the loss without comment. Chandler was excited, nervous and agitated out of all proportion to the reason he gave for his condition. If he believed his money was safe, the mere absence of an employee on a busy day would not, Brubacher thought, throw the man into so much mental turmoil. There was more to this than met the eye. But what?

Joseph Chandler had not killed a man across the street from one of his own undertaking shops. He had, he said, arrived early in the morning from Aiken, South Carolina. Brubacher would check up on that.

"Ain't you read the mornin' papers?"

"No. I haven't had time."

"Well, there was a guy killed last night, an' they brought 'im here."

"Yes?"

"Yeah, fellow from Trenton named Daniels."

"I—I don't know anything about it."

"One o' your men does."

2
MYSTERIOUS BUNDLE

BRISKLY, Patrolman Barnes entered the undertaking parlor. "You Brubacher?" he asked.

"Yeah."

"I'm Barnes. They gave me orders to see you."

"Yeah?"

"Yeah."

"Well, what happened?"

"It was before ten o'clock. I was on a corner. Up comes a short fellow with a yellow mustache and says the undertaker wants to see me."

Joe Chandler, seated at his desk, listened attentively.

"I didn't hold the guy. Why should I? I come over here. The door was locked, an' I pounded for a hell of a while before anybody come. Then a kid about eighteen or nineteen opens the door and says two guys just brought him a stiff. I didn't wait to look at it. I thought I better get the birds that found it. I chased two fellows in a cab, but it wasn't them. Then that fire started."

Brubacher turned to Chandler. "You got a kid workin' here nights?"

"Yes, Tommy Freeman. He's one of the night men."

"There's usually more than one?"

"There are two men on duty all night in each of the parlors."

"Go ahead."

"When the fire was out—near midnight—I came back here an' tried to get in. I pounded and rang the bell an' worried around an' called the desk for orders.

"The lieutenant says the morgue has the body, and the medical examiner will take care o' the case. All that I'm to do is look around at the scene o' the crime.

"Well, I didn't even remember where this kid said the body'd been found, exactly. But I found some blood stains in the freight entrance of the Bond Building. There's a fire exit in the same entry an' that door is standing open a little ways. So I dig up the watchman and we go up the steps."

"Across the street?"

"Yeah."

"Let's go over. We'll see you later, Mr. Chandler."

Reluctantly, the undertaker watched the detective and the patrolman cross the street and stand talking in the recessed doorway of the Bond Building. Fantastic visions moved before his eyes. How could this mix-up have occurred? Why had he to be entangled like this on the eve of his wedding?

He called his general manager on the phone.

"Send some one to take charge of No. 4. Some one who can keep his mouth shut."

Then he sent a telegram to his sweetheart, waiting for him in an Aiken hotel.

MISS JUNE WEISMULLER: Impossible to return, for goodness knows how long. Trouble here with employees and police. Do not worry, dear. Will be all right, but suggest you come to New York. Lovingly,

JOE.

He summoned his car, dismissed the chauffeur, and placed a soft, bulky bundle in the rear seat. He watched the rear door of the Bond Building for perhaps ten minutes. The two officers finally emerged and, to his immense relief, walked together to the street-car line.

The undertaker he had called for arrived very soon after the police had gone. Chandler drove nervously to Fifth Avenue, turned uptown and eventually took the Boston Post Road out of New York.

3
A KID STICKS HIS NOSE IN

A CONNECTICUT bumpkin sensed adventure in the parked bulk of the dark limousine. He burned a match, and, with the charred end, copied the license number carefully on the sleeve of his shirt.

Proceeding to the near-by bridge, he saw the owner of the car throwing heavy stones at a floating bundle—as if to sink it. Avoiding the man's detection, he crossed the road, down-stream, and followed the course of the bundle. The powerful motor started, and the car turned and started back to the city.

The boy retrieved the bundle from the stream.

4
TRY TO FIND CHARLEY!

BOTH Brubacher and Officer Barnes stood beside the marble slab which supported a dead man with a horribly mangled face.

"This guy was never murdered. He looks like he'd been in a wreck."

"But he was cleaned out. A button-hole on his vest is nipped—like his watch chain had been tore out. He didn't have a cent o' money, only a couple cards and receipts."

" 'At's easy. He was hit by a car. The driver got scared an' drove on. The body might o' been thrown into the doorway by the collision. Along comes a thief and goes through his clothes."

"That might be. Maybe the same guys that took 'im to Chandler's."

"An', maybe not. The boy that went through him ain't lettin' anybody see his face."

"That's true."

"Aw, nuts! If this guy was killed by a car how'd the blood get up four flights o' steps an' on the wash-room floor? Tell me that."

"I ain't a detective."

"An' where's his ol' lady? The boys in Trenton can't find 'er."

"She's missing."

"Uh-huh, an' so is eight thousan' smacks o' young Chandler's dough."

"The hell it is!"

"But he thinks Charley's got it for safekeepin'. But where's Charley?"

"I donno."

"Right!"

"Maybe that kid took the dough."

"Uh-huh! Even *I* thought o' that."

"Where you goin' now?"

"I'm gonna find Charley."

CHAPTER FOUR

1
THE WIDOW OF THE ILLUSTRIOUS CORPSE

THE widow of the wealthy attorney, Clark C. Macnaughton, left the next day on her palatial yacht for a Southern cruise. The widow's doctor had ordered the change directly after the funeral.

"You must get away from these memories as quickly as possible. Take a few congenial friends for the sake of your own health. It is not in the nature of a holiday, dear lady. It is medicine; very necessary medicine."

"Very well, doctor. You know best. I must get away. Oh, if I could only have seen his face once more! Just once more!"

"Please rid your mind of these thoughts. This dreadfully distressing circumstance must be put behind you. Come, start planning at once. I suggest that you take as many as four people with you and leave New York to-morrow."

2
IN THE HARDWARE STORE

IN Trenton, Pearlman was climbing another tree. With a local operative, he visited the hardware store owned by the late Frank Daniels. An old man greeted them with a lugubrious expression.

"Was Mrs. Daniels here yesterday?"

"She hasn't been in the store for months. Mr. Daniels wasn't the easiest man in the world to get along with, an' they were always fighting. She seldom came here. His uncle ain't been in the store for two years, an' it was his money started it."

"What's this uncle's name?"

"Robert Daniels. He lives in that big, red brick that sets back from the road as you turn off——"

"What's the address?"

"Well, I don't exactly know, but you can't miss it. It's the only big red——"

"What street?"

"Why, Chestnut Street. It'll be the corner of Chestnut and Locust."

"Got that?"

"Yeah."

"*You* wasn't in New York yesterday, was you?"

"Why, no, sir. I was here in the store."

"You have anything against Frank Daniels?"

"Why, no, sir. He—he and I may not have agreed always, but I had—had nothing against him."

"Pay you well?"

"Well, it was enough. I—I had asked for a little more, but business never seemed to warrant it. He was very good that way."

"Let's go see this uncle."

The worried old man followed them to the door. "What shall I do about the store? Shall I keep it open?"

The two detectives looked at each other for the answer. "What do you say?"

"I don't know. If we can find Mrs. Daniels, it's up to her."

"Suppose we wait till we see this uncle."

"All right. You stay here and sell washin' machines until you hear from us. We're gonna see this guy in the red brick that sets back from the road."

"Yes, sir."

3
MOUTH SHUT

BRUBACHER wanted the full names and addresses of the two men who should have been on duty in Chandler's chapel No. 4, the previous evening.

"I'm sorry, sir. But I couldn't give you that information. Mr. Chandler would have to get that for you at our main office. Naturally, no such records are kept in the various parlors."

"No?"

"No, sir."

"Um-hum! Where's Chandler live?"

"His home is on Long Island, sir. But he is not living there now. Since he returned from Aiken, he is in a hotel in the city."

"What hotel?"

"I can't tell you, sir."

"Never mind so much 'sir,' an' give me a little help here. Where's he livin'?"

"I don't know, sir."

"Aw, nuts. Do you know anything about eight thousand dollars being stolen from Chandler las' night?"

"No, sir. I hadn't heard that."

Joe Chandler had asked for a man who could keep his mouth shut. This one was certainly obeying orders.

"You know, I'm liable to pinch you, just to make you talk?"

"I wouldn't be able to answer your questions any better if I were under arrest."

"Aw, go roll a hoop."

Brubacher slammed the door.

4
STONE-WALL UNCLE

A SURLY old gentleman with white mutton chops granted Pearlman and his companion ten minutes.

"Be brief, gentlemen. Be brief."

"Your nephew's been murdered. You know that."

"Yes."

"Well, what do you know about it?"

"I know nothing about him or his affairs. I have not spoken to him in more than two years."

"A family quarrel?"

"Yes."

"Tell us about it."

"It's none of your business."

"Now, don't take that stand, Mr. Daniels. We want to find out who killed Frank Daniels."

"The notice I received seemed to indicate thieves. Why not let it go at that?"

"Do you know where his wife is?"

"I do not."

"She's left home."

"That's her business."

"Don't you think it's funny that she should disappear the day her husband is murdered?"

"I don't see anything 'funny' in murder."

"Well, ain't it peculiar?"

"I should say so."

"We want to find her."

"I can't help you. She is not here. We were not friends."

"No idea where she might've gone?"

"I can give you the address of her mother, I think."

"We been there. The old lady don't know where she is either."

"What do you want us to do with the body?"

"I don't care what you do with it."

"Now, look here, Mr. Daniels. You're the only relative Frank Daniels has—unless we can find his wife. You gotta do somethin' about the body."

"Very well. Send it to me. I'll bury it."

"That's more like it."

"What about the store?"

"What about it?"

"Do you want it kept open? The ol' man down there wants to know."

"Certainly, keep it open. It was my money that started that store. Naturally, it reverts to me."

"If his wife don't show up."

"Even if she does, the store is mine."

"You can settle that in court. Was you in New York yesterday?"

"I haven't been in New York City for five months."

"Was you there yesterday?"

"I was not."

"Is the mother of Mrs. Daniels the only relative or connection that you know of?"

"The only one."

"Did Frank Daniels have any brothers or sisters?"

"None."

"Parents alive?'

"No."

"My, you're talkative!"

"That will be about all, young man. I have nothing more to say."

"You know, there's ways to make you talk."

"I have answered all of your questions to the best of my ability. I have even given you permission to send the body here for burial. I can do no more. Good day!"

"Don't get so fresh. Can you prove where you were all day yesterday?"

"Leave this house instantly!"

The detectives gained the street.

5
MORE SILENCE

FROM the lobby of a hotel, Brubacher talked to Joe Chandler.

"My money was found, Mr. Brubacher. I found it myself; nothing was stolen."

"I'm glad to hear it. Now, what I want is the names and addresses of Charley and Tom, the two men in your place last night."

"You can get that from the main office."

"They won't give it to me."

"I will O. K. it for you in the morning."

"Can't you do it to-night?"

"All of the people there have gone home."

"Morning will be all right, then."

"Now, Mr. Brubacher, if there is anything else you want from me, you must ask it now, since I do not feel in any way responsible for any part of this affair and I will not want to be bothered about it any more."

"Don't you want to see these two fellows yourself?"

"Not at all. In any event, I would settle my affairs with them in private. I do not need the police to help me manage my employees."

"Well, I'll give you a ring when we get 'em."

"Don't bother, Mr. Brubacher. Good-by."

6
WIFE FLEES!

THE Trenton police and Pearlman forced their way into the Daniels bungalow. The lady had moved out, taking all of her clothing and many small personal effects. The neighbors must have seen her leaving. The neighbors were questioned. Yes, two trunks had been hauled away in the middle of the afternoon. Mrs. Daniels in a brown, tailored suit, had followed them within an hour in a hired car. The Daniels' car was locked in the garage.

The railroad attendants remembered Mrs. Daniels. She had signed a release for damages in excess of one hundred dollars each for her two trunks. She had gone to New York.

Pearlman telegraphed his findings to headquarters. The rechecking of the trunks in Grand Central was traced. Another trunk had been added to the two in New York. It had been delivered to the station by a small express line. The three had been checked to Chicago, and the receipt in this case was signed by a man—Henry O'Donnel.

Pearlman's orders were: "Proceed to Chicago! Find Mr. and Mrs. Henry O'Donnel!" The railroad company was asked to give Mr. Pearlman the name of the Chicago transfer company which claimed the three trunks.

In New York, a fledgling detective learned that the small express company had picked up the third trunk in the case at an uptown rooming house. Its owner had not been Henry O'Donnel then, but one by the name of Charles Everett.

7
A TRIANGLE?

AN item in the morning newspapers, October 5th, ran as follows:

POLICE SEEK MRS. DANIELS!
ROBBERY RUSE

Widow of Trenton Man Flees with Chandler Embalmer

Police to-day began a search for Mrs. Frank Daniels and Charles Everett, said to have left for Chicago yesterday, October 4th, directly after the identification of Frank Daniels' body.

The investigation of the murder of Frank Daniels, Trenton hardware merchant, took a new turn to-day when it was learned that the widow of the murdered man had fled her home on the afternoon of the crime.

Charles Everett, manager of Chandler's Undertaking Parlor, West Forty-fifth Street, where the body of Frank Daniels was later taken, is said to have accompanied Mrs. Daniels to Chicago.

Mr. Joseph Chandler, proprietor of the undertaking parlor, has refused to be interviewed.

8
A BULL

THEN Pearlman, in Chicago, pulled a boner which damned near cost him his job.

CHAPTER FIVE

1
SO!

BRUBACHER started for the home of Thomas Freeman. On a slip of paper in his pocket was the name of Charles Everett and his address. He went to the Freeman home first because Tom was the boy who had taken in the body. He was the only person Officer Barnes had seen there that night. Everett could wait.

Tom's mother was very worried. Tom had not been home for two nights. And he was such a good boy. Learning to be an undertaker, he was. Only nineteen and a fine boy. But he hadn't been home in two nights. What did the man want with him? Brubacher was only a man to the good old lady.

So far as she knew, she had never seen a detective before in her life. She could not imagine that her boy had become embroiled with the law. What did the man want with her son?

Brubacher hedged. It was something about his work. Would Mrs. Freeman call a certain telephone number if the boy came home, and ask for Mr. Brubacher?

Then he looked at the name of Charles Everett and his address.

Before the house lounged "Mack," the star of a big detective agency.

" 'Lo, Mack. How's tricks?"

"Pretty good! An' you?"

"So-so. Waitin' for Everett?"

"Yeah."

"Who put you on it? Chandler?"

"Uh-huh."

"I thought so. What's the charge?"

"I ain't heard. All I got is 'bring 'im in'."

"He's stole eight thousan' bucks from Chandler, the under-taker. You talk to anybody in here yet?"

"Not yet. Thought I'd wait around a while before givin' 'em a tip."

As they talked, the fledgling, flushed with discovery, came upon them.

"Hello, boys."

"Nuts." Two old heads resented this youngster's familiarity.

"Say, this guy Everett's gone to Chicago. He's changed his name to O'Donnel an' gone to Chicago with Mrs. Daniels."

Brubacher shook his head with mock gravity. "Yeah, I read the mornin' papers, too. Is 'at all you know?"

But Mack was surprised. "With the wife o' the dead guy?"

"Yes."

"It was in the papers."

"I found it out."

"*You* found it out, from a baggage check."

Mack's professional pride was hurt. "Is that what I'm workin' on? Another husband murder?"

"No, Mack. What you're workin' on is the loss of eight thousan' dollars. It's gone to Chicago, too."

"It's gonna be a big case," opined the fledgling.

"Big for you, but they come bigger."

Mack looked up at the number of the house. "Let's crash this."

The three men mounted the steps to the former residence of Charles Everett. Brubacher caught the young detective's arm. "You might as well go back to the station, sonny. You made one great discovery to-day."

2
SOME BONER

PEARLMAN, ignorant of the search for the missing undertakers, not yet informed of the real name of the man he sought, ran into Charley Everett in the hotel lobby in Chicago.

"Hello, Charley. What you doin' here?"

"Just passing through! And you?"

"I'm on a case."

"Yeah? What case?"

"This Daniels case. You read about it?"

"Yes. Some. What's the dope?"

"The wife has beat it with some guy an' is livin' in this hotel under an assumed name. I've got it narrowed down to four or five couples, but, like an idiot, I didn't bring any of her pictures with me."

"You sure they're here?"

"Sure. They came in yesterday, but I ain't sure who they are yet. But if they try to move, I've got 'em. The Parmelee man that delivered their trunks is ready to identify 'em if they try to take 'em out."

"Well, so long, Pearlman. See you again soon."

"So long, Charley."

And that is the conversation which nearly cost Pearlman his job.

Charley and Mrs. Daniels left the hotel without their trunks, within an hour, and were not heard of for a long time.

3
HEART AFFAIR OF A SLAVEY

THERE the case rested for a month. The Chicago police were requested to find Mrs. Daniels and Charley; Pearlman was taken off the case, and a half-hearted search for the Freeman boy continued without success.

The newspapers were asked to print as little as possible about the case, that the quarry might gain confidence and reveal themselves.

Then, as the reader has seen, Richard Roe revived the interest of the police and involved Sybil, a maid of neither pulchritude nor renown, who, in turn, sought the services of another roomer in the place, Raymond Fitzgerald.

Raymond was in the scenario department of a film company at a salary of what he referred to as: "Nothing a week, but they pay me in advance. So I manage to get by on it." He had been a newspaper reporter, had tried writing stories and scenarios and had eventually landed behind a battered roll-top desk where he cut good novels to pieces and patched them into successful motion pictures. He had more enemies among writers than any other man his age in the world. He made them rich by adapting their tales for the screen, but he left out all of their best scenes. At least, that was their plaint.

At the rooming house, his opinions were highly regarded. He was consulted on color combinations for new dresses, a choice of horses in the fourth to-morrow, whether an umbrella would be needed by midnight, and who it really was who shot and killed the two parties under the crab-apple tree. It was this last type of question which gave Sybil her idea of asking him to do what he could for the poor man no one knew.

Sybil accosted him as he was leaving his room for dinner.

"Mr. Raymond, may I talk to you a minute?"

"Not more than that, Sybil. As the good gray poet said, 'A woman waits for me'."

"Well, it's just this. They've arrested that poor man that I found and they're trying to say that he killed somebody."

"Who arrested him?"

"The police. They've got him in the station, and they won't let him go. One of the detectives was just here."

"Is that so? Just when you had him ready to propose, too."

"Oh, Mr. Fitzgerald, I never did." And Sybil tittered with pleasure. It was the first time in her life she had been twitted about a man. She loved it. "I only thought he was such a gentleman, and not being able to remember who he was or anything."

"They actually holding him?"

"Yes, they are."

"What did the detective say?"

"He asked if I was Sybil. I guess the poor man must have told him about me." She couldn't avoid a pleased smile.

Raymond nodded, smiling. "Of course."

"I said I was, and asked if he wouldn't sit down."

"And would he?"

"Oh, my, yes. He sat and asked me a thousand questions."

"And you answered them, of course."

"Why, certainly; he was a detective."

"H'm! Yes, sure. That would make a difference. What did you tell him?"

"I told him everything. How I'd found him wandering around that night and how I'd brought him here and everything."

"Uh-huh! And what did he say?"

"He asked: 'Did you know he had just killed a man before you found him?' And, of course, I said, 'No!' I didn't believe it. Do you believe it, Mr. Fitzgerald?"

That was a stopper. Like Brubacher, Fitzgerald had never believed in amnesia or aphasia. He thought the man was shamming or insane. He might or might not have killed a man just before Sybil found him. "Well, I wouldn't know that, Sybil. I hardly like to think so—especially when he's such a good friend of yours."

"Oh, Mr. Raymond, quit your fooling. Just think, they'll try to send him to the penitentiary or maybe the electric chair."

"Yeah, that's bad. Especially if he didn't do it. Who'd they say he killed?"

"He didn't say. But Mrs. Horn says the only murder that night was that man from Trenton on Forty-fifth Street, and sure enough"—the girl began to sob softly—"that's just where I found him. I'd just left the Hippodrome."

"Now, don't cry, Sybil. I'll see what I can do. I'll see what I can do."

"Oh, *will* you, Mr. Raymond? I—I know he didn't kill anybody. He—he couldn't."

"No, I guess not. Now, you just rest easy. I'll see what I can do."

4
RAY TAKES A HAND

RAYMOND told a beautiful companion of the strange circumstances surrounding the man in his rooming house, now in the hands of the police.

"You remember Sybil, the funny maid? Well, one night about a month ago, she went to the theater alone. She never has any fellows, you know."

"I shouldn't think so. I'm not naturally unkind, but a man would have to be nearly blind, I should imagine that——"

"That's just it. She looks like the wrong end of an all but fatal accident. Well, this night she comes up to my room about midnight and taps at the door and asks me if I will lend her an old suit of clothes. She says Mrs. Horn has just hired a new janitor and handy man and his clothes aren't very good and he needs a suit just to wear until he can get some.

"You remember that gray twill I had? Well, I was tired of it and it had seen better days, so I gave it to her. As time went on, by piecing fragments together, I gathered that she had found this dope wandering around on Sixth Avenue near Forty-fifth Street, dressed in a raincoat—and nothing more."

"Please!"

"Absolutely."

"Heavens! And he didn't get arrested?"

"No! Sybil coaxed him into a cab and drove him to the house. She smuggled him into the basement and got this suit from me. It didn't fit him, of course, but it covered him. Then she told old lady Horn she'd found her a janitor. The negro was sick at the time, and the bum fit in fine. You know, he could sweep, and lift things.

"Well, he claimed he couldn't remember who he was or where he came from or anything—and he took a shine to Sybil. Just now as I left, she tells me he's been pinched and charged with murder."

"No!"

"Absolutely. Adventure stalks into the house under my nose and I don't even know it. I thought he was just a dope, hiding out, or maybe some simple-minded bird that got away from his family. But, apparently, he is big guns."

"Who did he kill?"

"Wait a minute! You'll be sued for libel. He hasn't killed any one until it's proved before twelve good men and true."

"No, but I mean, whom do they think he killed?"

"Apparently, this fellow Daniels from Trenton. Remember? There's nothing much in the paper about it any more, but, a few weeks ago, they were hot after his wife who had disappeared the day of the crime."

"I remember now. His face was all hacked to pieces."

"You would remember that little detail."

"Is that the one?"

"Yes, I think so. I promised Sybil to find out what I could."

"Let's go over there now. We can see this picture another night."

"You don't care a whoop about my masterpiece. The best scenario ever written with a pair of scissors."

"I do, Ray, but can't we go to-morrow night? Heavens! Here's a real murderer, almost in the family."

"All right, all right. I'll swallow that insult. Joking aside, I would like to go and see what they're doing to the man."

"I'd love it. Where is he?"

"Uptown. I don't think he's actually been charged with the crime yet."

"Let's go. I never have seen an honest-to-goodness murderer."

CHAPTER SIX

1
COUNSEL FOR THE DEFENSE

THE police attempted to erect a case around Richard Roe. They gave him various versions of "the works." They told him he had killed Frank Daniels. He said: "Did I?" They told him he had been hired to do it by Charles Everett and Mrs. Frank Daniels! He said: "Was I?" And both times his questions were genuine attempts to learn something.

"You killed him with a sharp, jagged instrument—perhaps a dull hatchet or a box opener. What did you do with that instrument?"

"What instrument?"

"The hatchet."

"What hatchet?"

"The one you killed Frank Daniels with."

"Is Frank dead?"

"Did you know Frank Daniels?"

"The name is familiar."

"Why did you ask if he was dead?"

"And why call him 'Frank'?"

"Isn't that his name?"

"Isn't that whose name?"

"Frank's name."

"Yes. What's his last name? Quick!"

"Whose?"

Every one in the room heaved a heavy sigh except Richard Roe. Richard didn't bat an eye. His head was very much upset by all this questioning. He hadn't killed anybody. What the devil were they all talking about?

"Did you kill Frank Daniels?"

"No, sir."

"Where were you at eight-thirty on the evening of October 3rd?"

"I don't remember."

"Then how can you remember if you killed this man or not?"

"I can't."

"You did kill Frank Daniels."

"Did I? I didn't mean to."

"Then you admit you did it?"

"Well, you say I did. I don't even remember."

"You killed him with an ax."

"Did I?"

"Didn't you?"

"Couldn't anybody else have done it?"

"You did it."

"Well, maybe. I don't remember."

They gave up their questioning and sent poor Roe to sleep in his cell. "I wish you'd let me call Sybil. I certainly would like to see Sybil."

"You can see her to-morrow."

In his private office, the chief talked to Brubacher, Pearlman and Barnes.

"God, damn you, Izzy. If you hadn't let them get away from you in Chicago, we could burn the three of them. There ain't a shadow of a doubt. They hired this guy to kill Daniels."

"Chief, I didn't know you wanted Charley Everett. Nothin' was said to me about gettin' Charley Everett. I could of——"

"We didn't know we wanted him either, *then*. But you know it's your business to do your work without talkin'. Now we got to wait maybe another month before somebody turns 'em up again. An' there they were right in your hands. Now this guy walks in and gives himself up. Oh, what a bonehead."

"Say, but ain't it possible this express man got his calls mixed? How sure can we be that Charley Everett is O'Donnel in Grand Central and Pete Howell in Chicago?"

"Good Christ, it's a clear case. Him an' Daniels' old lady wanted to elope. They didn't have no dough. Everett goes through Chandler's safe, hires a dope to pound the life out o' Daniels an' they hop a rattler for Chicago. Y' can't get away from it.

"Here. Get these photos copied an' mailed to the Chicago police to-night." The chief handed two photographs of Mrs. Daniels to the man at his left. "Why didn't they send some photos of Daniels over here? Probably, the reporters stole 'em all, but I ain't seen any in the papers."

"What do you want photos of him for? He's dead."

"Well, I'd like to know what he looked like. You couldn't tell nothin' about that dead body."

An officer entered the room. "Two people want to see Roe."

"Who are they?"

"The fellow says he lives at the same address."

"Send 'em in."

Raymond and his beautiful companion entered the office.

"Good evening."

"What can we do for you?"

"I'd like to see this gentleman you are holding—the one who has lost his memory."

"Do you know him?"

"I live where he works."

"What is he—sort of janitor?"

"Yes, he's a general handy man."

"Do you know his name?"

"No, none of us know his name. Can we see him?"

"What do you want to see him about?"

"I'd like to find out what he thinks about being arrested. Ask him if he's guilty or not. Arrange for his defense."

"Are you a lawyer?"

"Yes."

The girl almost gave the lie away by turning to him in quick amazement when he answered in the affirmative.

"You his counsel?"

"I will be when I know what's going on. Has he been indicted?"

"Indicted for what?" The chief was attempting to be almost uncannily clever in this questioning.

"There was a detective at the house this afternoon who told the maid that this fellow had murdered some one."

"It ain't a formal charge yet. But you can't see 'im."

"Can't see 'im?"

"Nope. The jail's closed. You ain't been retained as counsel. You have to get a writ."

"What are you holding him for now?"

The chief didn't know. The lieutenant had booked the fellow. The question was really a blow below the belt.

"What do you mean, 'What am I holding him for'? He's suspected of murder."

"What's the charge?"

"Ain't that enough?"

"There must be something on the blotter."

"This is the detective bureau. I don't know what the police arrested him for."

"I'd like to find out."

"There's nobody stoppin' you."

"Good night, gentlemen."

"G'night."

In the hall, Ray grimaced at the girl. "We'll get a lot of help from that outfit! I've got to get busy. I'm going to free that poor duck now whether he's guilty or not just to make them sore."

2
ENTER DETECTIVE

THAT night, the young scenarist sat over a pad of paper until nearly dawn. He had talked with Sybil, had forced her by argument to tell him just what had happened the night she found Richard Roe. If she didn't tell him everything, her friend would be convicted, possibly electrocuted, he argued. She told him everything. Then he sat down to study.

All that he knew of the murder he had read in the papers. Briefly, their account had stated that Frank Daniels, a hardware merchant of Trenton, New Jersey, had been killed in a wash room on Forty-fifth Street with a jagged instrument which had obliterated his features. His body had been dragged down four flights of fire exit stairs and left in the freight entry of the Bond Building. Although robbery had at first seemed the only motive, the man's wife was known to have fled her home that same day. She had, in fact, been in New York City at the hour Daniels must have been killed. The police were seeking her. Meantime, the body had been sent to the man's uncle in Trenton who had buried it.

A later story told that the police were seeking, as her companion in flight, one Charles Everett, an undertaker until that time employed by Joseph Chandler, the wealthy young proprietor of a chain of undertaking parlors. Mr. Chandler could not be interviewed, but he admitted that Everett had left his employ suddenly.

Ray tried to see through the triangle. On its face, the crime seemed but a repetition of several similar husband killings, to make way for a new man. The police, apparently, were trying to prove that Mrs. Daniels and Everett had hired Richard Roe, an incompetent, to murder Daniels and to rob him to throw the authorities off the scent.

If this were true, where was the money they had paid Roe? Where was the money and the watch it was known Daniels carried? And where were Roe's clothes? Why would a murderer wander about only a block from the scene of his crime, in only a raincoat, merely a few hours after he had done a man to death? Even if he were crazy, it was illogical.

Yet the man could not have traveled far, clad in only a raincoat, without attracting attention.

Where was the raincoat? That seemed the only vestige of identification poor Richard Roe could offer.

The first question seemed to be: Who is Richard Roe and what made him that way?

Raymond put down these notes and went to bed:

Look at raincoat for possible clews as to Richard Roe's true identity.

Buy newspapers with first story of the crime.

Look Roe over for possible bumps or cuts on head which may have caused loss of memory.

Follow Frank Daniels' every step from the time he was known to decide to come to New York until his burial back in Trenton.

3
WHAT DID ROE SEE?

An item in the morning papers of November 7th ran as follows:

APHASIA VICTIM KNEW OF
DANIELS MURDER

———

Nameless Man Leads Police to Scene of Crime

The mysterious murder of Frank Daniels on October 3rd seemed nearer solution to-day than at any time during the prolonged investigation. An unidentified man wearing borrowed clothing gave himself up to-day, disclosing details of the crime that, it is alleged, indicate he was either a witness or an actual participator in the murder and robbery of the Trenton hardware magnate. He claims to have lost his memory on or about October 3rd.

CHAPTER SEVEN

1
BLOODY MONEY

MEANWHILE, in Stamford, Connecticut, young Al Palmer was creating some stir by his sudden affluence. There seemed to be no end to the boy's money. He bought a suit of clothes, a new hat, four neckties, and a pair of shoes. He wore a gold watch with a "hunting" case, and he treated his crowd to ice cream and the movies. He bought his girl a beaded bag and a lace handkerchief. His funds seemed inexhaustible.

His father took him in the woodshed and glowered down on him.

"Now where the devil are you gettin' all this money? Huh? Where you gettin' it?"

"Well, I'm workin'. I saved it."

"Saved! You're lying, an' I know it. Come on, cough up! Where's it comin' from?"

"Well, I won some of it, playing cards."

"Gamblin', huh? Goin' to the dogs an' gamblin'. How much'd you win?"

"I won a hundred dollars."

"A hundred dollars! Who'd you play with?"

"I played with the fellows, I did. An' I won a hundred dollars."

"Where'd you get that watch?"

"I won it on a bet."

"A bet, huh? Turned out a better, huh? Let me see it!"

"No."

"Lemme see that watch!"

There was no denying that tone of voice.

"Who'ja win it from?"

"From a fellow."

"Al, you're lyin' to me. I don't believe you won the money nor the watch. I think you're doin' somethin' y'hadn' oughta."

"I ain't stealing nothin', dad. I ain't stole a cent. I found 'em all right an——"

"Oho! Y'found 'em now, hey? Where'd y' find 'em?"

"I found 'em in the creek over toward Darien."

"In the creek, huh? Y'found a good gold watch and a hundred dollars in the creek, huh?"

"I did so. But there was more'n a hundred dollars. There was two hundred."

"Al, you're lyin' again, ain't you?"

"So help me, I ain't dad. I found 'em."

"Al, I'm gonna beat you black an' blue, big as you are, unless you tell me true where you got that money."

"Dad, I am tellin' the truth. I found it in the creek."

"I don't believe it." The elder Palmer started to roll up his sleeves. "I don't believe it, and I'm gonna pound the truth out of you if it takes all night."

"Aw right, dad. I'll tell you. I'll tell you the whole thing. The truth is there was seven hundred and forty-three dollars."

That gave the elder Palmer pause. There was something convincing about the odd figure named which almost offset the enormity of the sum.

"Seven hundred and forty-three dollars!"

"Yes, sir, and fifty-six cents."

"Seven hun—an' the watch?"

"Yes, sir, in a suit of clothes wrapped up in a bundle."

"Honest, son?"

"Yes, sir. An' I didn't tell you 'cause I was afraid you'd make me give the money back!"

"Give it back? Then you surely stole it!"

"No, I didn't, dad. I found it, like I'm tellin' you. I found it in this bundle in the creek."

"When'd you find it?"

"I found it near a month ago."

"Where's the suit?"

"I buried it."

"Where'd you bury it?"

"Out back."

"Dig it up."

Al started for the shovel.

"How could I make you give it back? Who's it belong to?"

"I don't know."

"Then how could you give it back? How much of it y'got left?"

"I got more'n five hundred left. But I ain't gonna give it back. The man threw it away himself."

"Who threw it away?"

"Well, a man in a big car threw it away."

"Threw away more'n seven hundred dollars?"

"Well, he did. I saw him."

"Dig up the clothes."

Al dug in the soft earth back of the shed and in a pit, slightly mildewed, were a disreputable coat and a pair of trousers.

"Al, have you killed a man?"

Al began to cry. "I ain't done nothin'. I was comin' home, an', after I'd crossed the bridge, I saw this big car standin' by the road with nobody in it an' I saw it was a New York license and I wondered where the guy was. I looked around an' he was over by some elder, throwin' rocks at a package in the water, an' I waited till he'd gone away, an' I went an' fetched the package, an' these clothes were in it, an' the money an' watch were in the linin'. Y'can see it was all tore."

"Y' tellin' the truth, Al?"

" 'At's the truth, dad. An' I buried the clothes an' began usin' the money. That man must not 'a' wanted 'em or he wouldn't of thrown 'em in the creek."

"That man had killed somebody, Al. He was destroyin' the evidence."

"Why didn't he keep the money then?"

"Come along, son, we're goin' to the police. Y' got the rest o' that money?"

"Yes, sir."

"Let's see it."

"Y'ain't gonna make me give it back, are you, dad?"

"You're darn tootin' I am. That money's got blood on it."

2
HORRIBLE!

Young Chandler's fiancée, June Weismuller, plucked at her program, waiting for him to return between the acts. He settled himself beside her with a nervous little laugh. "Sorry, dear. I seem to be smoking a lot lately."

"I've noticed it. You never used to leave between the acts."

"No. I've got to shut down. During the day, I must race through two or three packages."

"That's too many. And that's not the only indication of nerves that I've seen lately."

Joe was startled. "No? Do I act nervous? Have you noticed it?"

"Noticed it? Why, Joe, you jump out of your skin—at nothing. You're distraught. What's the matter?"

"Nothing. Nothing. I guess it's just the same old thing. Sick to death of this infernal under-taking business. My, how I hate it! What a way to make money! It's horrible."

"I thought you meant to get out."

"Out? Of course, I mean to get out. Just as soon as I can possibly get some one to buy the business. It's too big for one man to buy. Dad built up the largest chain of undertaking parlors in the world, I guess. I wish they were bakeries or pool rooms or something—anything but what they are."

The theater was darkened, and the play progressed. At its close, they drove to a night club for something to eat.

"Are the police still bothering you, Joe?"

"No. Why did you ask that?" His voice was hard, filled with quick alarm.

"Oooh, you're so touchy. I was interested, of course, and asked because I know there's something worrying you. You're actually becoming petulant."

"June, I'm sorry. I don't mean to be. I beg your pardon. I'm all unstrung. You see, the police have dug up some chap now, whom they claim was hired by Mrs. Daniels and my man Everett to kill Daniels. It's such a rotten mess."

"But why do they bother you with it? You never even saw this man Daniels. They had taken him from your place before you were even in New York City."

"Oh, I wish that were true."

"Well, isn't it?"

"Oh, yes, yes, of course. I mean, I wish they could see that."

"Joe, darling, what are you hiding from me? What is making those lines come around your mouth? Why do you never play as you used to?"

"Oh, June, I'm a criminal. I've committed a crime that I never heard of before. Something new in the police records, as far as I know. I don't know whom I harmed by it. I don't know if there is a punishment on the statute books to cover it. But I dare not confess; I dare not tell any one what I have done."

"Why, Joe!"

"Trust me, June. For Heaven's sake, trust me. I was beside myself. I didn't know what I was doing. And I made one idiotic blunder that has made this detective, Brubacher, suspicious of me."

"What did you do?"

"The blunder? I told him eight thousand dollars had been stolen from me that night. It was true. The money was gone. But I didn't want them looking for it. It would have been dangerous to have them looking for it. Dangerous to me. At least, I thought it would. Guilty conscience, likely.

"Next day, when I told him I'd found the money, he didn't believe me. I told him I would have nothing more to say to the police. He thought I was lying, though he can't understand why. Now that they have this imbecile, they are coming around again, and Brubacher has the effrontery to twit me about the eight thousand. Says he never knew such a good loser in his life—and the like."

"What was the terrible crime you committed? Why haven't you told me this before?"

"I can't bear to talk about it. I can't even tell you now. I'm leaving for a long sail to-morrow. Perhaps sea air will give me courage. Won't you trust me, and love me, without that?"

"Of course, I'll love you. Who could help it! But confession is good for the soul."

"I suppose I could tell you. But it's too grisly. No, I can't!"

3
A CLUE

RAY turned over his private collection of "clues": A complete set of New York daily newspapers dated October 4th, the day after the murder; an old raincoat, much too small for Richard Roe and a letter taken from the raincoat pocket. The letter was addressed to Tom Freeman, postmarked from Butler, Pennsylvania. It was a simple note from a simple boy to his pal.

> DEAR TOM: I was glad to get your letter and glad to hear you could get away so soon. Dad is going away on the first of October, and I will be alone with mother. She says she will be glad to have you any time then, if your mother says you can. So why don't you get her to write to her that it is all right?
>
> There was a big party last night at Phylis' birthday, and there is another one next week at the twins' house. I wish you could be here, and we would have a good time. I'll tell the world. So why don't you hurry up and come?
>
> Very truly yours,
>
> EDDY.

Young Ray Fitzgerald put the letter down and turned again to the newspapers. "The body was taken to Chandler's Undertaking Parlor." In an adjacent column: "The funeral will be from Chandler's chapel." The illustrious Macnaughton funeral. "The many friends of the late Clark C. Macnaughton will be unable to view the remains since the tragic accident which took his life also mutilated the great man's features."

Something in the young man's mind clicked as he read that line. Mutilated features! He took one of the afternoon papers. "A jagged instrument had been used, because the man's features were mutilated beyond recognition." And in another: "It was thought at first that the man had been the victim of an automobile crash, but a crimson trail up the steps to a fourth floor wash room in the Bond Building revealed that Mr. Daniels had been the victim of foul play."

The telephone on the ground floor of the old brownstone began a monotonous summons. Ray started down the steps. *Two* mutilated faces in the same undertaking shop the same day. *Two* men who could not be recognized by their faces! After all, with Frank Daniels' wife away, who had identified his body?

"Hello."

"Hello, Ray?"

"Yes, Jake? How are you?"

"Fine. Listen, Ray, I been thinkin' since you called me up. Can you keep still about some dope?"

"Yes, sure."

"Well, you know the police got the old man to lay low on this Daniels story because they wanted to pinch Mrs. Daniels."

"You told me that."

"Well, we haven't been printing much, but we've been working just the same. All the papers have been asked to lay off, but they've all got men on it."

"Yes."

"Well, a friend o' mine in Stamford just tipped me off that some kid up there has got a watch with 'F. D.' on it that he claims he found with a lot o' money. The old man in the hardware store in Trenton gave us a description of the watch Daniels was wearing, and I'm getting a train to Stamford in an hour. You want to come along?"

"I should say I do. What else?"

"I'll tell you the rest when I see you. I'm leaving Grand Central at four thirty."

"Well, wait. I've got a clue I'm working on. A letter. I'm going to call at this address, and I'll get on that train at One Hundred and Twenty-fifth Street."

"All right. I'll be in the smoker."

Ray hung up. Daniels' watch in Stamford! Two men without faces! Tommy Freeman's raincoat. The first job was to learn who Tommy Freeman was. Second, to catch the train.

He made a bundle of the raincoat and took a cab to the address on the letter.

Mrs. Freeman answered his knock.

"Is Tommy home?"

"Now, who are you?" The good old lady burst into a flood of tears. "Every day it's a new one. Every day it's somebody else. You all know my boy's not home. You all know where he is, but you won't tell me. Go away and let me alone, or tell me where my boy's gone to."

"Are you Tommy's mother?"

"I am. Oh, please, mister, if you know where the lad is, won't you tell me? What's he done? Is he in jail? I can stand to know. What's he done?"

"I don't know that he's done anything. How old was Tommy, Mrs. Freeman?"

"He was twenty, come May."

"Only twenty." That eliminated Richard Roe; he was nearer fifty.

"An' so industrious."

"Where did he work?"

"Honest, don't you know? They've been making game of me for near a month now till I'm nearly frantic. Come in, young man. Come in an' sit down."

Ray looked at his watch as he followed the old lady into a shabby, genteel living room of the late '90s. He had nearly an hour.

"Is this Tommy's coat, Mrs. Freeman?"

"Why, yes, so it is. Where did you get that, now?"

"A man was wearing it. Mrs. Freeman, will you believe me if I tell you that I want to be your friend? That I want to help you find Tommy?"

"Well, they've been so funny, all of 'em. They come an' question me an' threaten me, an' all I want on earth is to see my boy again, safe and sound. Somebody's kidnaped him, that's what."

Ray produced the boyish letter. "Do you know who wrote this?"

Her spectacles located in the kitchen, Mrs. Freeman read the letter. "Oh! Do you think he's there? But he would of written to me. He always writes to me. He didn't mention goin' there. He never even asked me."

"If you will give me the full name and address of this boy, I'll find out if he's there, Mrs. Freeman."

She sought the address, talking the while. "You knew he was working at Chandler's, learning to be an embalmer, an' he was smart at it, too. Then, the very night that man was killed, he went away. I haven't seen him. Here is the address of Edward Coleman. You can take this with you."

"Thank you, Mrs. Freeman, and, if you don't mind, I'll keep the raincoat, too. You see, I don't know what Tommy can tell me, but—but he might know a lot."

Ray's thoughts were incoherent. Tommy was an embalmer's apprentice. His raincoat must have been in Chandler's. Then Richard Roe must have been without clothes in Chandler's. Why would a living man be without clothes in an undertaking parlor? Roe's memory gone! The possibilities were amazing.

Ray left the Freeman household after a few more questions and dashed to the station to join his newspaper friend on the train.

CHAPTER EIGHT

1
FIND THE WEAPON

BRUBACHER was charged with the duty of finding the deadly weapon Richard Roe had used to chop up the face and head of Frank Daniels. He went about it skeptically, without hope. Five weeks! Five weeks after the murder, he should go out and pick up the murder hatchet! What did they take him for? Hadn't he been over every inch of that building twenty times?

He talked once more to the engineer of the building.

"That fire exit opens from the inside only. Your man must have been in the building, and the murderer, too, before six o'clock."

"Well, what was Daniels doing in the building? We've questioned every office in the place and nobody ever heard of him. What have you got on the fourth floor? A manufacturing jeweler, a tailor, a publisher, the office of the building and commercial art studio. I've been to 'em all. An' not one of 'em has any Daniels whatsoever on their lists.

"Now you just tell me what the devil was he doing in the building in the first place?"

"I don't know. But he must of been here. That blood didn't crawl up them steps by itself. Was the door locked when you got here?"

"I didn't come on the case until the next day."

"Did the cop say it was locked?"

"I don't know. He might of got your night watchman to let him in."

"That door is always securely locked. They must of been in the building all night."

"Well, where's the weapon? What did he kill him with an' what did he do with his clothes?"

"Who, this nut you pinched?"

"Yes."

"He never had nothin' to do with it. He's a squirrel."

"Well, where'd he come from at that hour of the evening without no clothes on? We got that baby dead to rights. He was found on the corner here, right after the murder, by a woman. She took him home with 'er, an' then, a month later, he turns up with this fish story about seein' visions."

"I heard o' them guys before. An' you think he's the guy that done it, eh?"

"No question. But what did he do with the money, the weapon and his own clothes?"

"I give up."

2
WRITTEN TO ORDER

In his home, Doctor Evansborough, medical examiner, was having a bad half hour with his conscience. He was trying to explain to himself how he had come to write that report in the Daniels killing. As he looked again at the body, in retrospect, he could not imagine what weapon could possibly have been used to dispatch the fellow. Some of those cuts had been made by glass.

What could they expect? Dig him out of bed at four in the morning. Tell him the body had been dragged down four flights of steps. Point out that the face had been hacked and chopped! Why, he was half asleep. He had agreed with them. "Killed with a dull hatchet or similar instrument." It had been easy to think that then. Now he was sure that the body he examined had been in an accident. But how could he reverse his findings? How could he claim, weeks later, that he had made a mistake. It would mean his job. He would be discredited and removed. Why had he let his judgment be warped by circumstances they described? Why had he not based his opinion solely upon the evidence offered by the body itself?

Now they were attempting to make a case against this incompetent. Basing their deductions on the report he had signed. Why, if they tried and convicted the fellow, *he* would be responsible. *He* would have—might have—been responsible for the punishment of an innocent man. But they couldn't convict Richard Roe. Even if they proved he had committed the murder they could only confine him in an asylum, and perhaps that was the place for him, innocent or guilty.

But they would find the wife—and her lover. They would try them. Those two were not insane. The law might send them to the electric chair. All because he had been sleepy and had allowed the suggestions of others to blind his professional sight. What a mess! Could he change his report? After all, wasn't it accurate? If it should be proved that the man had been killed in an auto accident, couldn't his report be interpreted broadly enough to cover that? "A dull hatchet or similar instrument." The idea—when some of these cuts obviously had been made by glass!

Well, who could he tell it to? The chief of detectives? Brubacher? They wouldn't listen now. They were satisfied with the thing working out exactly as it was. They had wanted the report they got that night. They had suggested, almost dictated it to him. It was a much simpler case this way. How could they reconcile the victim of an auto accident with that trail of crimson up the steps? No. They were happy with the report. They wouldn't let him change it if his changes increased the mystery. And it had been a long time ago. Perhaps he was wrong. Perhaps those were not glass cuts.

But the wounds had not been fresh. They had been washed, almost treated—as if the body had been partially prepared for burial.

3
THE BUMPKIN TELLS

THE Stamford police felt no animosity toward the press. They had nothing to conceal from the public. They were not directly connected with the case. They were even a little flattered at the visit from the two big city reporters and a photographer.

Jacobs introduced Ray as a fellow news gatherer. The bumpkin was summoned. The watch, money and clothing were produced. Together they examined the articles; together they reviewed the boy's story.

"I got the guy's license number."

For a moment, this information stunned the entire group. He had the license number of that car? He held the entire secret of the crime, and, apparently, he had not regarded the fact as of any importance!

"You what?"

"I got the license number o' the car."

"For God's sake, what is it?" Jacobs bellowed.

From his pocket, the boy produced a dirty slip of paper. "I wrote it on my shirt sleeve an' copied it."

"The movies are a great teacher," Ray murmured.

Jake laughed. "Can you imagine that?"

The police chief was more serious. "Why didn't you tell us this before, young man?"

"I dunno. Here it is."

Jake copied the number quickly. "This is the biggest thing yet. That's a direct lead. Let me see that watch again." He copied the number of the watch movement and made a sketch of the case. "Boy, you may be famous in a few days. Will you stand over there while I take a picture? Here, hold up these clothes."

Al held the ragged suit against him, and the photographer exploded a flash light.

"You might as well shoot the watch, too, Doug. It'll all come in handy."

Then the group drove to the creek where the bundle had been found, and Doug used up all his negatives. Al Palmer was caused to open a bundle at the exact spot he had opened the real one. He was caused to register amazement as he plucked money from the torn lining of the ragged coat. His signature was affixed to an instrument giving Jacobs the right to retell the story in his own way, and the three men boarded a train back to the city.

On the train, Jake pledged himself to inform Ray of his every move. "We aren't going to release this stuff at once. We're going to try to get the whole story together first, then spring it an' make the police look like a tramp. You know: 'Acting on information given them by a *Record* reporter, the police to-day apprehended—' etc. It's great for the circulation."

"What will you do first? Find out whose car that was?"

"Sure. I can get that dope in ten minutes. Then I'll act accordingly. You can come along, if you like."

"But I've got another lead." Ray produced the letter he carried. "I'm taking a train to Butler at once."

"Why not wire?"

"That might scare the kid."

"Right. Better go. Who's financing you?"

"I told the boss I was working on something that would be good for us, and he's staking me."

"Great. You heard about the eight thousand, didn't you?"

"No. What eight thousand?"

"Why, Brubacher, the dick, says that Chandler lost eight thousand dollars the night o' the murder. One o' those two birds took it. Either Everett or this kid, Tommy Freeman."

"This seven hundred couldn't be any part of that. Whose clothes are those, anyway? You suppose they're Richard Roe's? They can't be Daniels' even if his watch was in 'em. His were sent to Jersey with the body. Don't you suppose?"

"Well, Chandler told Brubacher that he found the money later. Nobody believed him. Maybe those were Richard Roe's clothes. My God, Ray, maybe that guy *did* kill Daniels. He's missing a suit. He's suspected of the crime. Here's a suit without an owner, with evidence that the guy that wore it stole—at least, the watch. If those rags fit your friend Roe, it'll be tough to clear him."

"Unless the owner of the auto talks."

"Talks! Man, he'll have to talk. I only hope I can get to him before the police do. Let's see. It's eight o'clock now. If the Stamford authorities don't telegraph New York, I'll beat them to it. And I'll telegraph you at Butler."

CHAPTER NINE

1
SYBIL GIVES

SYBIL drew her savings—fruit of thirty years' incessant labor, at beds, at floors, at pots and pans—from the bank and left it with a professional bondsman who secured Richard Roe's release.

Her mouse-colored hair straggled in wisps too homely to be called "scolding locks", from the edge of her home-made hat. She was indulging in a cab again, the first since she had taken this man home.

"Mr. Ray is working for us, Richard. He has got his office to let him."

"Gee, that's fine. That's great. Gee, you're good to me. Everybody's good to me. You got me out of jail and—and everything."

"Well, we—we like you, Richard. Mr. Ray an' I both like you."

"I like—like you, both, too, Sybil. But, gee, I—I don't even know who I am or nothin'. Is Mr. Ray gonna try to find that out, too?"

"Yeah, he's tryin'. He's awful smart, Richard."

"Yeah, I know he is. I bet he even knows if I killed that man or not. Do you suppose he does?"

"I don't know. We'll ask 'im when we get home. Don't *you* know?"

"Gosh, no. I don't know anythin'. Say, I guess I should 'a' told him about my feelin' instead o' the police, but I never thought."

"What feeling? What do you mean?"

"Well, about this fellow bein' killed. Honest, now, I think somebody got hurt there in that place."

"What place? What are you talking about? Do you know where the man was murdered? Oh, Richard, *did* you do it?"

"Oh, I don't know. I don't know. Oh, my head aches, Sybil. It's just fit to split right now."

"I'll buy you some aspirin."

2
BLOOD STAINS

PROUDLY, Brubacher unwrapped a package on the desk of his chief.

"There y'are—with dark stains on it—an' hair."

"Where'd you get it?"

"It was in the engine room o' the Bond Building."

A rusty wrench lay among the crumbled sheets of paper.

"It could 'a' been that."

"Sure it could."

"Well, what'll we do? Give it to the chemist?"

"I guess so. Better dust it for prints."

The wrench was subjected to every conceivable test. Finger prints were found in abundance. The prints of the Bond Building's engineer—and the blood proved to be that of full-grown rats, as, also, was the hair.

3
THE PROPOSITION

THE telephone of the Assistant District Attorney Frisbee rang as he dictated a letter to the Chicago police department.

"This is Frisbee."

"This is Alexander Black. I am an attorney, Mr. Frisbee, attorney for Mrs. Frank Daniels."

"Oh, yes, Mr. Black." The State official became attentive at once.

"I've called to tell you that my client is innocent of any complicity in the murder of her husband."

"I'm glad to hear it, Mr. Black. Won't you come over and discuss this matter with me in person?"

"Surely. When shall I——"

"Come right away. I'll be here for hours."

"I'll be right over."

"Be seated, Mr. Black."

"Thank you."

"You—you say you are convinced that Mrs. Daniels had nothing to do with this murder?"

"I can prove her innocence. That is why I called you. She had communicated with me, confessing every detail of her—shall I say—er—indiscretion? She has asked my advice, and I have given it to her, subsequently getting her permission to make this proposition to you."

"Proposition?" The representative of a State could scarcely be expected to listen to "propositions."

"That I—offer these suggestions," he emended.

"Quite so."

"Mrs. Daniels will be glad to appear here for questioning. Will come back and answer your every question if she is assured that no one will press her prosecution for any crime save complicity in the murder of her husband."

"I don't quite understand you, Mr. Black."

"It is just this, Mr. Frisbee, Mrs. Daniels is conscious of having broken certain laws, but she has not committed murder nor has she had any hand in it. We can prove her innocence on that score, but it would be equally easy for you to prove her guilty of less important offenses. Do you understand?"

"Well, perhaps."

"If you will guarantee her immunity from any other charge, she will be glad to aid you in finding the person who killed her husband. Naturally, she is anxious to settle his estate."

"Naturally."

"Well?"

"How about Everett? Will you produce him, too?"

"I am not Mr. Everett's attorney. I speak only for Mrs. Daniels."

"Well, they're together, aren't they?"

"I do not know."

"Where is Mrs. Daniels?"

"Is it a bargain?"

"How about Everett?"

"I might ask her," Black said with a smile. "He might—er—get in touch with her. She might be able to persuade him to come here on the same basis."

"Same basis! I don't want him on that basis. We've got another count against him that can't be quashed."

"I don't understand."

"Never mind. Chandler understands. It was his money."

"You mean there is some money missing from the undertaking parlor?"

"Only eight thousand dollars."

"Is that all?"

"I hope you don't think Chandler is going to forget that overnight."

"Not likely. Well, I hadn't heard about that. Nothing has been said about that, nor about Everett at all, for that matter."

"Well, Mr. Black, I'm afraid I'll have to arrest your client without your permission. I can't agree to your terms."

"Very well, sir. Good day."

"Um-hum! Good day."

4
BY WIRE

JAKE's telegram to Ray Fitzgerald in Butler, Pennsylvania, was never received by the young writer. He had left Butler an hour after his arrival, acting on information from the elderly mother of Tommy's friend. His ticket was for Philadelphia. The undelivered telegram read:

License owned by Joseph Chandler, millionaire undertaker. Laugh that off.

JAKE.

CHAPTER TEN

1
TOM IS FOUND

DESPITE a fund of information in the hands of both the newspapers and the police, the morning newspapers on December second carried not one line of news regarding the murder of Frank Daniels.

In a cheap rooming house in Philadelphia, Tommy Freeman and Ray Fitzgerald guzzled gin and sang bawdy songs. More accurately, Tommy drank, and Ray sang. He was breaking down the younger boy's suspicions. It had been a long, arduous process, but it was at last producing results. Tommy was beginning to trust him. He was talking. Even when he was sober, he was talking.

Ray had secured a job in the neckties at a department store to strengthen his background with the boy. He railed against policemen and sought to draw out similar outbursts from Tommy which might contain some evidence. Finally, he so far convinced the boy of his guilelessness that they became fast friends, roommates. Day by day the story grew. Evening by evening Tommy added to the pattern of facts which Ray needed to round out the theory he was convinced could not be wrong.

Like a tapestry, slowly fashioned by hand, the picture grew, disclosing the events of the night of October third, and revealing the real murderer.

2
DEEP SEA FLIRTATION

Off Bimini, at proximitous anchorages, rode the private yachts of Joseph Chandler and Mrs. Clark C. Macnaughton. The dainty *Naiïd* strained at her cables to rub the romantic side of the *San Malo,* but that old reprobate of the sea rolled leeward with a shrug for such flattery.

They rode thus, flirting, courting, playing—until Joe learned whose ship the *San Malo* was. Then steam was ordered and New York marked as their destination.

The *Naiïd,* feeling her master's hand, threw her heels high and raised her dainty nose as she was put about past the adamantine *San Malo.*

3
FROM THE GRAVE

On December eighth, Brubacher sat at the desk of the assistant district attorney, with his chin in his palm. "As far as I can see, nobody cares who killed Frank Daniels."

"*I* do. Election's coming on."

"I never thought o' that. But, outside o' you, nobody cares."

"But it will be the seventh unsolved murder in less than a year unless we catch somebody. That can't go on."

The telephone rang.

The lawyer answered, then handed the phone to Brubacher.

The chief's voice came over the wire. "Go over to Trenton as quick as your feet will let you. Phillips is in the station over there, claimin' he seen Daniels."

"What?"

"He says he seen Daniels not two hours ago. Either him or his ghost. Go on over there, quick!"

"Who's Phillips?"

"The old man in the store."

"The old guy in the hardware store?"

"Yeah. He says Daniels came an' stood in front o' the store for a few minutes an' then ran like hell."

"You want me to go over there?"

"Yes. Get the first train."

CHAPTER ELEVEN

1
SEVEN DISAPPOINTED MEN

A BIG black touring car drew to a halt before a bungalow on Lockwood Avenue in Oak Park, Illinois, suburb of Chicago. From its overflowing tonneau two men, with black sticks under their arms, alighted and ran silently around the little house to the rear. A third man with his hand in his overcoat pocket sauntered a few feet to the south of the house. A fourth man, this one also with a shining stick, walked a rod to the north. A fifth man crossed the street. A six and a seventh man clumped up the steps to the porch.

The car stood empty, thirty seconds after its arrival. The house was completely surrounded.

A warm, yellow light streamed from the living-room window. A man and woman could be seen at their dinner in the dining room beyond.

One man rang the bell. His companion, looking through the window, saw the couple start, rise and turn quizzical eyes toward the front of the house. They came to the door together.

"Ready, boys!"

Gruff voices grunted. The shining sticks were then held in readiness. One man took his hand from his coat pocket, and a sliver of silver light flashed from the nickeled barrel of a revolver. Their feet shuffled in preparation—for anything.

The door opened.

"Good evening," said the first caller. "Sorry to disturb your dinner. You two people will have to come with me."

"Cha—John!" the lady cried and clung to her companion's neck.

"Who are you?" asked the householder, much calmer outwardly than his companion.

"We're police officers, and we have a warrant for the arrest of Mrs. Beatrice Daniels and Mr. Charles Everett, alias Mr. and Mrs. John Carter. Will you come along or will there be monkey business?"

"What is the charge?"

"Well, this paper says you are wanted in New York State to answer a criminal charge filed on the strength of some claims of the Atlantic Insurance Co."

"The Atlantic Insurance Co.!"

"Yes, ma'am. Seems your lawyer has collected insurance from them on a man that ain't dead."

"Mr. Daniels?"

"I guess so. You want to get your coats now?"

The men with the sticks put them rather sulkily into the car and held on as the driver took them rapidly toward the loop. It was a devil of a man hunt when you didn't get a chance to so much as pull a trigger. You could tell these people were from New York, all right. Make it plain to them they had *criminal* charges to answer. They must know they could be sent to the pen. Tell them exactly how serious it was, and they don't even lift a finger in their own defense! Boy, try that on a native of Cook County!

2
ROE SKIPS

"What do you mean by letting a maniac out on bond? Who told you you could do that? That man's a dangerous criminal. He should be in an asylum—and you let him out—to run around and kill other people? He's a fiend. He's a menace to the community. Rearrest him immediately and bring him here." Frisbee was upset. Richard Roe was a fiend! And Richard Roe was, to date, the only arrest in the Daniels case.

Police swept down upon Sybil as she dusted the parlor chairs. "Where's this Richard Roe?"

Punctuating her answer with emphatic swipes of her oil-soaked cloth, Sybil answered. "He's gone! He's run away."

"Come on, none o' that. Where's this bird hidin'? Where's 'is room?"

"His room's in the basement, you wise guy. Go see for yourself. But you won't find him. He's skipped his bond, I tell you. An' left me—all alone."

The detectives searched the house, but Richard was not to be found. Bond or no bond, the adult waif had wandered off, leaving Sybil without a bank account.

3
TOM GETS AWAY

JAKE, of the *Record,* read a telegram that Ray had sent.

Meet me at the Pennsylvania Station twelve sharp.

RAY.

He was there when the train arrived from Philadelphia.

"Listen, Jake. This is Tom Freeman."

Jacobs noticed for the first time that Ray was not alone. He shook the slender, bony hand of the youth with a feeling of repulsion. "How do you do?"

"Pleased t' meetcha."

"Tom is going home, Jake. You're to take him there. And nobody is to see you go in. Most especially, the police. Don't let a cop get near him. And don't print anything he tells you. I've got a lead that I'm following or I'd take him home myself. God knows his mother is going to think you're an angel when she sees you with this kid."

"Your mother's been awful worried about you, Tommy," said Jake.

"Yeah, I know it. But I'm goin' back now. That'll make up for it."

"What's your lead, Ray?"

"I'm going uptown to visit some people who don't expect me. And I may not get in. But if I do—and if I find out what I think I'm going to find out—the *Record* will have a front-page story to-morrow that will knock them dead!"

"What is it?"

"I'm going to the home of the guy that crashed Frank Daniels' skull."

"The hell you are!"

"I'd like to say 'come along'; but I can't. I want a friend with Tommy."

"I'll take care of him, but——"

"You're the only one I could trust with Tommy. I don't want him pinched, and I don't want the cops to know he's back."

"I'll get him home. Then where can I find you?"

"Stay in your office. I'll call you there later to-night. Here's some cash." He handed Jake a one-dollar bill in which was folded a note. Turning, Jake read:

Don't let him get out of your sight. When you've left him with his mother, wait outside the house. I'll meet you there.

"So long, Tom. You'll be all right with your mother, and I'll come to see you to-morrow."

"Good-by, Ray. You're honestly comin' back for me?"

"Sure I am. An' don't worry. You'll be all O. K. with Jake. Jake's my pal. But, remember, once you're inside, don't leave the house until you hear from me."

"I won't, Ray. I'll stay inside."

"Don't worry about us, Ray. We'll get along all right. Come on, Tommy."

Ray took an uptown express subway. Jake bundled Tom in a cab.

"Well, your mother will certainly be glad to see you, Tom."

"Yeah, poor ma. I never meant t' stay away like this, but I was scared to come back."

The reporter in Jake was always master of the man. "What were you scared of?"

"Ray told me not to talk."

"He didn't say you shouldn't talk to me, did he?"

"Yeah, he said most specially you."

"The bum! After all the tips I've given him."

"He's a fine fellah."

"Yeah, he's great. Why shouldn't you talk to me? I'm not going to do anything to hurt either one of you."

"I guess you couldn't do anything to hurt Ray."

"Oh, no? I'll bust him in the nose."

"Ho, I guess you won't."

"Oh, won't I? The double crosser!"

"Ray Fitzgerald never double crossed nobody. He's the best scout I ever met in my whole life. An' I know my way home by myself. You get the hell out o' this cab. Hey!" He rapped on the window. "Stop here."

"No! Never mind! Go where I told you!"

Now another idea, typical of a reporter, careened across Jake's mind. Tom was important as a witness. Ray told him not to talk.

"I was only kidding, Tom. If Ray told you not to talk, he's right. You do what he told you. You don't mind stopping at my house for a minute, do you? I want to pick up my flask."

The boy shrugged sullenly. Jake changed the address with the chauffeur and relaxed in the corner of the cab. At the door to his apartment, Jake invited Tom to have a drink.

"Come on up. It'll only take a minute."

Tom followed him silently.

In the apartment, Jake contrived to get the boy in his bedroom, and to lock him in quickly. "I'll be back in a minute," he called, and dashed to the street.

It was a seventh-floor apartment, but Tom was thoroughly frightened. This was not the treatment Ray had promised him; this Jake was holding him, perhaps calling the police. He raised the window and looked out. There was no way out. He scrutinized the walls of the court. He might be able to grasp the kitchen window. It was worth the attempt. Like a fly, he crawled across the smooth face of the building, just able to touch one sill from the next.

In the kitchen, he was no better off. The hall door was locked from without. He picked up the telephone, then replaced it. The dumbwaiter!

He opened the slide door and pulled experimentally at the rope. The car responded. Slowly, he moved the little box closer to his hand. Then, breathing a silent prayer to whatever pulleys or wheels revolved above him, he sat on the serving contrivance and slowly descended, hand over hand, the rough rope tearing his palms.

4
BACK TO ANSWER FOR AN UNTOLD CRIME

His wireless operator handed Joe Chandler a message as he stood watching the water swirl in anger behind the shapely *Naiïd*. It was signed by his attorney.

> Advise immediate return. Criminal action started by insurance company. Goldman and Irving ready to sign.
>
> BLANCHARD.

Joe entered the salon and picked up the telephone. "The captain, please."

"Captain Ayers, speaking."

"This is Joe, captain."

"Yes, sir."

"Get back to New York as quickly as possible. Let's have all the speed you can get."

"Aye, aye, sir."

In the bowels of the yacht, bells rang. A startled engineer scowled in bewilderment. There was no accounting for the whims of a millionaire. It was bad luck to ship on an undertaker's barge, anyway.

Three minutes later the *Naiïd* was doing better than thirty knots, straight toward the Goddess of Liberty.

"Criminal action!" What did that mean? What "insurance company"? Action against whom?

But, happy day! "Goldman and Irving ready to sign." That was news for which he would have crossed half the world. He would be rid of those undertaking shops. He would be free. He could marry—he could live—unless the police interfered. What investigations would this criminal action start? How could he stop them?

Could he buy an insurance company? Could his money secure him immunity? If it could not—could he—face the music?

Under his feet, the *Naiïd* throbbed in perfect rhythm, carrying him closer and yet closer to a reckoning.

5
THE PRESS

THE morning newspapers, December ninth, read as follows:

FRANK DANIELS ALIVE

"DEAD" MAN REPORTED
SEEN IN TRENTON

John Phillips, manager of the Daniels Hardware Co, of Trenton, told the police that, at about five o'clock last evening his employer, reported murdered and supposedly buried in Brookside Cemetery, Trenton, stood before the store for a full minute, peering in the window.

When Phillips approached the front of the store, he says the man fled. The police immediately threw a dragnet over the city and posted guards at the Daniels home and the home of Mr. Robert Daniels, the uncle of the supposed victim of foul play.

In another column:

DANIELS WITNESS FOUND

MISSING UNDERTAKER RETURNS
THEN DISAPPEARS AGAIN

The *Record* to-day located the missing undertaker's assistant, who has been sought since October third as a material witness in the mysterious murder of Frank Daniels, Trenton hardware man.

Tommy Freeman, formerly employed by Chandler's undertaking parlors, was recognized to-day as he alighted from a Philadelphia train. A *Record* reporter failed in his attempt to turn the young man over to the police, but followed him for a considerable distance and talked to him.

"My lawyer has told me to say nothing," said young Mr. Freeman. "I have nothing to say."

In another column:

LONG-ESTABLISHED FIRM OF MORTICIANS TO CHANGE HANDS

Mr. Joseph Chandler is expected to arrive in New York to-morrow to complete negotiations for the sale of his entire chain of undertaking parlors to——

In still another column:

STATE SEEKS TO EXHUME DANIELS' BODY

TRENTON OFFICIALS TO ACT TO-MORROW

Henderson Frisbee, of the district-attorney's office, today indicated that the body of Frank Daniels, murdered hardware merchant of Trenton, New Jersey, would be exhumed to throw light on several points now but vaguely understood. Although the situation seemed portentous, Mr. Frisbee refused to disclose what he expected to learn from the coffin buried nearly two months ago.

CHAPTER TWELVE

1
TOO MUCH HASTE

AN irate elder in a sporty vest hammered the conference table in the board room of the Atlantic Insurance Company. "You young fool," he roared. "You young idiot. Where the devil did you study law? I'm out of town three days and you get this company involved in the worst case of—of——What the devil do you mean, sir? Do you know that this case may cost us a million dollars? Do you?"

"We will win the case, Mr. Jeffries."

"You can't win it. All you've got to go on is the testimony of an old fool who saw a ghost. And you start criminal action."

"I have already told you that I was acting upon advice from the State. Willard and I went over it all very carefully. The only way we can lose the case is by having them prove that Daniels is dead, and, if they prove that hard enough, they'll prove themselves guilty of the murder. And that's just what Frisbee wants—it won't cost us anything."

"Bosh! You shouldn't have moved until the body was exhumed."

"They were planning to get away again."

"They could have been watched. See here, young man. The State can't prove that Frank Daniels is alive. Neither can it prove that those two people had any hand in the killing. If they had any evidence to prove that, they would have indicted them months ago."

"It was our man that found them. The police didn't know where they were."

"Oh!" The old man sighed in dramatic resignation. "Are you an idiot? They were arrested two hours after you telegraphed. When will they dig that body up? The sooner I know the worst, the better."

"The Trenton police are at the cemetery now. Our man is there. The uncle and the wife are there."

"Why the devil aren't *you* there? You started this thing. Why don't you see it through? Are you afraid of a dead body?"

"Mr. Jeffries, I am a lawyer. My place is at the bar, not in a morgue."

"Your place is in the nut house. And if you think you're a lawyer, let me see you get us out of this jam. Mind you, if you lose a dollar of this company's money, you'll have to go to work to earn a living, for, so help me, you'll never make another dime at the practice of law!"

2
WHOSE CORPSE?

GENTLY, Mrs. Frank Daniels cuddled her slim shoulders into the protecting arm of Charley Everett. Jake stood next to them at the side of the rough box. At its foot, old Phillips, the manager of the hardware store, wiped his forehead. Two reporters flanked him; the emissary of the insurance company stood next. Glowering down at the long, pine box on the other side, stood Robert Daniels between two uniformed policemen. The medical examiner, Brubacher, another doctor, and still more reporters and news photographers clustered at the head of the moldy carton. The room was filled with detectives, police and gentlemen of the press.

A representative of the district attorney's office nodded to the medical examiner. The officials fidgeted. This was something new to each of them, and they pretended to each other that they had been through it all many times before. The medical examiner cleared his throat.

"You may open the—the—it—you may open it, gentlemen."

The sexton of the cemetery and a local undertaker unscrewed the pine lid. Taking fresh courage, they applied themselves to the head board of the plain black casket.

"Oh!" The widow shuddered. "Isn't there any way to stop this? Uncle Robert, for Heaven's sake, didn't you look at him before he was buried? Didn't you even see him?"

The old man shook his parchment mask from side to side and lowered his sandy brows to conceal his eyes still further.

The board came off.

Those behind the ringside spectators pushed with concerted energy to get a better view. A photographer from a New York tabloid set off a flash light. A policeman swore and tried to take the camera.

Mrs. Daniels, nauseated, hid her head on Everett's shoulder. Charley's eyes opened wider and yet wider. No one spoke. The fellow from the insurance company finally looked at the two people who were there—indirectly—at his behest.

Charley sputtered. "Why—why, for Christ's sake, that—that's Clark C. Macnaughton!"

3
CHANDLER SELLS

IN the offices of Blanchard & Train, Attorneys at Law, several bundles of gold bonds had just changed hands; several signatures and handclasps had been exchanged, and the principals arose to go.

Mr. Irving waved both hands on a level with his shoulders. "Veil, Mr. Chandler, you certainly got a fancy price. You certainly did."

"And you got a splendid property, Mr. Irving. I'm sure you don't feel that you have paid more than the business is worth."

"No-o-o, maybe not. I'll tell you, young man. My bardner and me talk it ofer, and ve agree dat d'good vill is vort more than anything else. Chandler's got a fine reputation."

"Yes, it certainly has."

"Vell, good-py."

"Good-by, Mr. Irving. Good-by, Mr. Goldman. Good-by."

The two new proprietors of Chandler's undertaking parlors closed the door behind them.

Joe raised his arms in the air. "Thank God!"

"You surely wanted to get rid of the business, didn't you, Joe?"

"I should say I did. Oh, I'm glad that's over, Blanchard. Will you take care of this deposit for me? I'm going to take June out in the country somewhere and get married to celebrate." He picked up the telephone.

"Main 0982.... You're welcome."

The lawyer cleared the bonds and legal documents from the table.

"June, darling. It's all over. I've sold out, and I'm a free man. Will you marry me to-night?"

"I'll marry you this afternoon."

"We'll drive to—to—oh, anywhere we aren't known. Shall we?"

"Fine."

"I'm coming right up after you. Pack a light bag. I've got the roadster."

"Righto."

"So long, Blanchard. See you next week."

At the foot of the steps, a man with flat feet and an extremely puffy nose accosted Mr. Chandler. "Mr. Chandler? I'll have to ask you to come along with me. The distric' attorney'd like t' ask y' a few questions."

"The district attorney?"

"Yes, sir. The same."

"But what does he want to ask me?"

"He didn't say."

"May I telephone?"

"Sure thing! Sure thing! You ain't pinched. You are merely asked to grant us the courtesy of an immediate call."

"Oh, I see."

"That's all."

"In that case, suppose I go back upstairs and get my attorney. Perhaps I'll be asked questions I shouldn't answer."

The operative shrugged his fat shoulders. "Who can tell?"

Joe bounded into the office. "Blanchard! I've been summoned to the district attorney's office. Come along."

"Why, what's the matter, Joe?"

"I—I'm not sure. Come along! Can you?"

"Certainly."

"Main 0982. Yes, yes, yes! Oh, for Pete's sake, hurry up! Hello, darling. No! Miss June, please. Hello, darling, listen, dear. I won't be right up. I've been delayed. I'll call you again—perhaps an hour. I must run along now. Don't worry. Good-by!"

CHAPTER THIRTEEN

1
THE SOREHEAD

MRS. FREEMAN answered her telephone the moment it rang.

"This is Raymond, Mrs. Freeman. Any news from Tommy?"

"Well, no, Raymond. No news."

"Hasn't he called you again?"

"No. He only called that once. He ain't run away again, has he, Raymond?"

"No, I wouldn't say he ran away, Mrs. Freeman. I guess he's just waiting for word from me. You know, I told him not to use the telephone very much because certain people tap wires and listen in."

"Well, Raymond, you might let him call me up once a day, anyway, so's I'd know he's all right."

"Yes, I guess I could do that. Well, thank you, Mrs. Freeman."

"Don't mention it, my boy."

Ray hung up. "I wonder if that old lady is putting something over on me. I wonder if that fool kid is there. She'd rather die than give him up."

Then he called the *Record*.

"Mr. Jacobs?"

"Mr. Jacobs isn't in."

"Will you tell him Ray Fitzgerald called?"

"Yes, sir."

"This is the fifth time I've left that message, and he hasn't called me back in three days."

"I gave him the message myself, every time, Mr. Fitzgerald."

"Are you sure?"

"Positive."

"Maybe he doesn't want to call me."

"Maybe not."

"Well, will you make it a point to see that he gets this message? Then if he doesn't call me, I'll know it's because he doesn't want to talk to me."

"Yes, sir."

"I'll call you again to-morrow."

"Yes, sir."

Ray left the telephone booth and went to the Bond Building. He got off the elevator at the fourth floor. He sauntered down the corridor, glancing at the doors as he passed. He entered the little wash room at the end of the hall and scrutinized it carefully. He went around to the dimly lighted fire exit and walked down the four flights of steps. Then he ascended them. He found himself locked in the fire stairway. The door from each floor gave easy access to the steps, but no one could enter any part of the building from those steps. Ray pursed his lips and, whistling softly, again descended to the street.

He went up in the elevator again, taking care that a different operator drove the car. At the fourth floor, he again alighted and went straight to the manufacturing jeweler. He found himself in a cubicle partitioned off from the rest of the firm's floor space with high ceiling, opaque walls. A tiny window framed the frizzy bobbed head of a typist.

"Can I help you?" she asked without the least desire to know.

"I'd like to speak to the manager or the owner of this establishment."

"Is it about some merchandise?"

"No, it's a private matter."

"I'll have to know the nature of your business."

"It's about your vault."

"The vault?"

"The vault."

"Jus' a minute. What's the name, please?"

"Fitzgerald."

"Fitzgerald?"

"Fitzgerald."

"Just a minute." The head disappeared.

A few moments later, a chain lock was released and a lock turned. A narrow door opened, and the dumpy girl said: "Will you step this way, sir?"

At the end of a short hall, the girl knocked at another door. A sliding panel was opened by yet another young lady of the same general cast of features. "Mr. Fitzgerald to see Mr. Bloom."

The eyes behind the sliding panel searched Ray for concealed weapons. Then, slowly, the door opened and shut behind him with a mechanical click.

Such caution, he thought! Dealers in gold and precious stones. Took him for a holdup man. He was admitted to the presence of a short, plump and bearded man in carefully cut business clothes.

"How do you do?"

"Yes, sir. Something about the vault?"

The man's tone itself was suspicious.

"About October first, you had the combination of your vault altered so that no one without the new combination could possibly open it. Is that true?"

"Just a minute, young man. Who am I speaking to, please?"

Ray smiled disarmingly. "Mr. Bloom, I'll tell you. On the night of October third, a man was murdered in the wash room on this floor. I am a detective, looking for information on that case."

"The police have already been here twenty times. We don't know anything about it. Daniels, the name. We got no Daniels."

"But I want to know why you had the combinations of your vaults and safes changed, just before that murder?"

"How could it be anything about it? How could it?"

"It may have nothing to do with it, Mr. Bloom. And yet, it may. Surely, it can do you no harm to tell me why you made that change."

"Well, I guess not. I guess not. All right, I'll tell you. It's this fellow we fired. He's no good. He's stealing all the time. He makes trouble with the workingmen. He wants they should strike. He knows the combinations. He has the keys. He's been here a long time. I fire him. I know he's sorehead. I figure some trouble." Mr. Bloom shrugged. "So I change the combinations so he can't take nothing."

"Was that man's name Sigmund Ladensky?"

"Yes, that's him."

"And did he live at 404 Plymouth Avenue?"

"That's the man. That's the man. Say! You think he done it? Huh? You think he killed this fellow?"

"We don't know. We're just looking around."

"Say, he was a bad egg. I wouldn't put nothin' past that fellow. What a bum!"

"All right, thank you, Mr. Bloom. If I want to see you again, will it be all right?"

"Yeah, sure. You just tell the girl. I'll remember you, young man. You just tell the girl."

"Good-by."

"Good-by, my boy. Good-by."

Ray crossed the hall to the tailor's. "Are you the proprietor?"

"Yes, sir."

"I'm a detective."

"Oy! Again it comes."

"Did you ever see this pattern before?" From his pocket, the young man produced a four-inch square of suiting, soiled and old.

"Now, I should remember. Boys! Who could remember this piece of goods?" Four tailors hung over the sample for a few moments.

"Yeah, sure it is. I remember."

"It's funny, mister. This suit, we remember. This suit was made up for a man from Chicago. Then he goes away without it. Oh, more than a year ago. He don't come for it. It hangs here. Then we sell it for next to nothing to a fellow across the hall; he ain't here no more."

"You sold it to one of the jewelers?"

"Yah. One of the jewelers. A big fellow. He got fired."

"Sigmund."

"Yah, that's right, to Sigmund."

"All right, gentlemen. Thank you very much. Good day."

"Yah, good-by."

Ray whistled softly to himself as he waited for the elevator. Now, if he could only find Tommy again!

2
THE ILLUSTRIOUS CORPSE

The late afternoon papers, December 10th, ran as follows:

EMBALMER IDENTIFIES BODY

———

CLARK C. MACNAUGHTON FOUND IN DANIELS' GRAVE

———

When the coffin supposed to contain the body of Frank Daniels was opened in Trenton to-day, it was found to contain the remains of Clark C. Macnaughton, prominent New York attorney, the victim of an auto accident on October second.

The body was identified by Mr. Charles Everett, an embalmer formerly employed in Chandler's undertaking parlor No. 4. Mr. Everett said: "I could not very well be mistaken. This is indubitably the body given into my custody by the hospital authorities on October third. I washed those wounds myself, attempting to make it possible for friends and relatives of Mr. Macnaughton to view his remains.

"The last I saw of this body it was on an embalming table in Chandler's undertaking parlor."

CHAPTER FOURTEEN

1
THE STATE HAS A THEORY

IN the office of the assistant district attorney sat Alexander Black, attorney for Mrs. Daniels; the young man named Carr; Mrs. Daniels herself; Charles Everett; Brubacher and the assistant district attorney. Mrs. Daniels wept softly.

The door opened, and the man with the puffy nose led Joe Chandler and his attorney into the room. The State's representative rose. "How do you do, Mr. Chandler?"

"How do you do? How do you do, Mr. Everett?"

"Hello, Mr. Chandler."

"You're quite a stranger," the young millionaire said.

"Yes, I—I've been away."

"I noticed that."

Frisbee, the ambitious, the only one, according to Brubacher, who was interested in who killed Frank Daniels, introduced himself to Chandler.

The young man nodded. "This is my lawyer, Mr. Blanchard."

"Mr. Blanchard."

"Mr. Frisbee."

"This is Mrs. Daniels."

"How do you do?"

"Mr. Carr."

"Mr. Black."

"Mr. Brubacher, the detective in charge of the case."

"Mr. Brubacher and I have met before."

"Yeah," said Brubacher. "One time I thought I might find some money Mr. Chandler lost. But he found it himself."

"Yes," Chandler said, looking not at Brubacher, but at Everett. "I found it—myself."

Charley had not yet met his former employer's eyes.

"Well, Mr. Chandler," Frisbee said in his official voice, "we are confronted with a very peculiar set of circumstances. I might say the most unique set of circumstances it has ever been my misfortune to encounter. Will you smoke?"

"No, thank you."

"We have to-day—that is, the Trenton authorities have to-day exhumed the remains of what every one, I imagine, had thought was Mr. Frank Daniels." He inhaled deeply of his cigarette, then continued talking as the smoke curled from his mouth and nostrils. "They found that the coffin contained, not the body of Frank Daniels at all, but the body of my—of our"—with his head gallantly including all the legal talent present—"illustrious colleague, attorney Clark C. Macnaughton."

"Oh!" Chandler exclaimed. "In Jersey?"

"Yes, sir. In Jersey. Now, that is a very strange circumstance, and we are attempting to arrive at some explanation. Understand, please, that I am making no accusations. I have no charges to make at this time. I feel, as the servant of the State of New York, that we can here, between ourselves, arrive at some understanding without bitter words or recriminations. Excuse me." He picked up the telephone. "Beulah, please ask the sheriff to detail three men at my door. At once, please. Yes. That's right." He replaced the receiver and went on.

"The State, rather—the police department, represented by Mr. Brubacher and his assistants, have been attempting to solve a murder mystery ever since the night of October third, last.

"So far, little progress has been made. The police have met open hostility at every turn. Please excuse me, Mr. Chandler, but even you have not given us the support we might expect from a loyal, law-abiding citizen of New York. But you were not alone in your attitude of 'let the cops find out what they can; it's none of my business'. Not at all. That seems to have been the general attitude everywhere.

"Even now, Mr. Daniels' uncle has refused to come to this conference. He refused to view the body when it was delivered to him for burial. Only the greatest pressure was sufficient to get him to the cemetery to-day for the purpose of identifying his nephew. If he had looked at the body when it was first sent to Trenton, we might not now be in such a tangle. The murderer of Frank Daniels might even now be on his way to the electric chair."

"If," Lawyer Carr interposed, "if Frank Daniels has been murdered."

"Quite right, young man. If Frank Daniels has been murdered.

"Right there, we are at a loss. Has Frank Daniels been murdered?"

Joe Chandler started to speak, but Blanchard's hand slid out to contract on his wrist and the monologue was resumed.

"Let me state the case briefly. On October third, last, Mr. Daniels left his home in Trenton to come to New York City to collect a debt of more than seven hundred dollars from a business acquaintance on lower Manhattan. Mr. Daniels made that call and collected that money. Who saw him collect that money;

who may have followed him, we do not know. He left the office of that man at approximately four thirty in the afternoon of October third.

"Now, Mr. Everett tells us that he had been an old friend of both Mr. and Mrs. Daniels for a period of years. He says that, on the day of the supposed tragedy, about five thirty or just before six o'clock——Am I right, Mr. Everett?"

Charley nodded. "That's right."

"Just before six o'clock, Mr. Daniels came into the place of his employ, that is, your undertaking establishment, Mr. Chandler, to pay him a friendly visit.

"Now it is alleged by Mrs. Daniels that she and her husband had not been happy together for several years. It is alleged that they quarreled repeatedly and that there were scenes both in private and in public. It is also alleged that Mrs. Daniels and Mr. Everett had discussed the possibility of her leaving her husband. Had discussed the likelihood of their being happier with each other, than in their present, at that time, condition. Mr. Everett is a bachelor.

"They had even discussed and, I may say, set upon a day when they should—er—elope together. That is, they had planned to run away the first time Mr. Daniels gave them an opportunity to do so without a bitter scene."

"At my expense!" young Chandler blurted.

"We are not here to make accusations, Mr. Chandler. If you will note carefully, everything I have said thus far is susceptible of proof. All of of it is from informal testimony, and none of it is in the nature of—er—criminal libel?

"No, I shouldn't mention the loss of any money, if I were you, Mr. Chandler."

"Excuse me, I'm sorry."

"You found it, anyway, you know." This from Brubacher!

"Is there any law against killing detectives?"

"Now, Mr. Chandler. I would advise you to avoid rancor. Your social prominence and great wealth are without meaning before the law, and the State has a few questions to ask you and——"

"He needn't answer them, you know," said Blanchard with elevated brows.

"No, quite right, Mr. Blanchard. He needn't answer them. Not here. But probably Mr. Chandler would rather tell us here without a court stenographer just why he drove so far into Connecticut alone on the afternoon of October fourth, last—

"Yes, I imagine from Mr. Chandler's expression that he would rather explain that to us here than in a crowded court room before a—jury?"

"Are you attempting to intimidate my client?" Blanchard yelled.

A shadow of a pair of broad shoulders darkened the glass in the hall door.

Frisbee cleared his throat. "Not at all. I am simply suggesting that we will get a great deal further with our inquiry if we all remain friends."

"In that case, Mr. District Attorney, please instruct that cheap detective to keep his insolent mouth shut."

"Do you refer to Mr. Brubacher?"

"Yes, Mr. Brubacher." Chandler was behaving like a spoiled child. He reversed the position of his crossed legs with a jerky, nervous flounce.

"Mr. Brubacher, will you please help us out by allowing for the inconvenience some of these people are suffering to be here with us? It is our business to be here, yours and mine, but they have other business and I imagine a meeting of this kind is very annoying to them."

"I'm shut."

Mr. Frisbee sighed. "Where was I? Oh, yes. Mr. Everett and Mrs. Daniels planned to leave this part of the country, perhaps go out West and start anew, the first time Daniels—er—Mr. Daniels left her alone. There is a telephone record of a long-distance call from the Daniels home in Trenton to your undertaking parlor at about noon of October third. This, we assume, was from Mrs. Daniels to Mr. Everett, saying that Mr. Daniels was in New York. Do you mind telling us exactly what you said over the telephone that day, Mrs. Daniels? Mind, you don't have to."

"I got Mr. Everett and told him Frank had gone. He said 'fine,' that he'd meet me at Grand Central at seven o'clock. I figured that Mr. Daniels would be on his way back to Trenton by that time. I think that is all that was said."

"Was anything said about Mr. Daniels calling on Mr. Everett that day?"

"Oh, yes. I said: 'He'll probably come in to see you.' And Charley said that——"

"Yes?"

"Charley said——"

"Yes?"

"I said: 'If he comes in here, I'll put him in one of Chandler's satin-lined kimonos.' That's what I said."

Beatrice became very agitated. "But it was just a joke, Mr. Frisbee. Like anybody says those things. He didn't mean he was going to kill him."

"No, no, my dear. Of course not. We all say those things. Luckily, we don't all do them." The man's smile was gelid.

"Well, I felt that way about him. I'll admit that. He was a beast and I——"

Frisbee raised his hand. "Never mind, Mr. Everett. If you wish to dictate a confession, I'll just call a stenographer and have you sign it so these people can go home."

"I'm not malting a confession. I didn't kill him."

"Well, then, let us get on with our story. At any rate, Mr. Daniels did call at the undertaking parlor that afternoon, directly across the street from the place he was murdered."

Mr. Carr cleared his throat.

"Yes, yes, Mr. Carr. Granting, of course, that the man is dead. Don't forget, Mr. Carr, that there was more than one dead body in Chandler's undertaking parlor on October third. Just because you didn't find the man in a Trenton cemetery doesn't mean that he isn't dead. We may have to dig up a few more graves. Eh, Mr. Chandler?"

Joe glared at the cool, taunting gray eyes without speaking.

"Do you mind telling us what took place at your meeting with Mr. Daniels on that afternoon, Mr. Everett?"

"He came in, and we shook hands. He asked me when I was coming out to see them. I said I didn't know; that we were pretty busy. We talked along about the election and the weather. He said he was going to catch his train and left. He wasn't in the place more than twenty minutes. The moment he was gone, I left, too."

"Leaving another employee, young Mr. Freeman, in the parlor alone?"

"Yes, sir."

"Did you, by any chance, take along a bundle of bank notes belonging to Mr. Chandler—er—perhaps for safekeeping?"

"I did not. They were in the safe. I knew they were there. They were to be banked the next day, but we knew Mr. Chandler was coming home from Aiken, and we held them overnight so that, if he wanted ready cash for anything in the morning, he could get it without trouble. We always handled it that way."

"How did you know Mr. Chandler was coming home from Aiken?"

"He telegraphed me."

"Why?"

"Because of the Macnaughton funeral."

"Do you always travel so far for an important funeral, Mr. Chandler?"

"I usually try to be present at a funeral of that magnitude."

"How did you know Clark C. Macnaughton was dead?"

"Mr. Everett telegraphed me."

"Did you know Clark C. Macnaughton by sight before his death?"

"I——" Joe turned, undecided, to Blanchard. "That's——"

Blanchard shook his head. "Don't answer un less you want to, Joe."

"All right. I refuse to answer that question."

Frisbee nodded vigorously. "Do you appreciate, Mr. Chandler, that none of these other people have seen fit to refuse to answer the questions I have put to them? Do you realize that you at once cast suspicion upon your fairness in this matter?"

"You may proceed with your inquiry, Frisbee. My client doesn't want to answer that one either."

"When was Mr. Macnaughton's body taken into your chapel, Mr. Everett?"

"About five o'clock the day before."

"Where did it come from."

"We got it from the Accident Hospital. He was taken there from his car after the crash."

"And he was badly cut?"

"There was practically no face left. He was dead when they took him from the wreckage."

"And you didn't embalm that body?"

"No, sir. Since the body could not be viewed in the casket, it was not necessary to do a particularly careful job, so I turned it over to the apprentice, Tommy Freeman. He worked around with it trying to fix up the face that first night. I helped him at that. He was going to embalm it the night before the funeral."

"And when you left him alone with the Macnaughton body, you didn't care what became of him or the body or Frank Daniels or the chapel or anything."

"That's about it. When this opportunity came for Bea and me to go away, I didn't think of anything else." He reached for her hand and held it very tightly.

"And you, Mr. Chandler, were rushing back here from Aiken to see that everything went off well at the funeral of a famous man. Is that it?"

"Yes, sir."

"Did you know at that time that Mr. Macnaughton's face had been horribly mutilated?"

"No, sir. I did not."

"And to-day, Mr. Everett, when you looked at the body in New Jersey, you were positive that that body was the same one you received from the Accident Hospital and not another one with a mangled face?"

"I'm positive. I studied the cuts very closely to see if anything could be done so that Mrs. Macnaughton, at least, could see her husband again."

"Then it is your contention that you left the undertaking parlor at about six o'clock on the evening of October third?"

"Yes, sir."

"And never returned to it?"

"Never."

"Where did you go?"

"I took a cab to my room, packed my trunk and a bag. Left word for an expressman to come for the trunk and then rushed to Grand Central."

"There you met Mrs. Daniels?"

"Yes, sir."

"And then?"

"We—we went to a hotel after buying tickets to Chicago."

"You registered as man and wife at a New York hotel?"

"Yes, sir."

"What hotel?"

"Is that necessary?"

"Well, no. Perhaps not right now. It will be, later. Do you remember the name you used?"

"Yes, sir."

"Then that will be easy to check. Did you stay in your room all evening?"

"I refused to answer."

"There's that idea again. Don't you people realize that you get right down to a salient question—one that has very direct bearing on the case—then you refuse to answer? What's wrong with you? Do you all want to go to jail?"

"My client resents that remark," said Alexander Black.

"Oh, let her resent it. My God, Black. Did they stay in the room or did they go to a show? I've got to know. The man was killed before nine thirty."

"Can't help it, Frisbee. Chivalry demands silence."

"Chivalry! This court is just as chivalrous as any court in the United States——"

"What do you mean, 'court'?"

"Excuse me. I'm getting ahead of myself. Then, Mr. Everett, in the morning, did you not read of the crime in the morning papers? Did you not know when you boarded the train for Chicago that the husband of that woman was lying dead in the morgue?"

Carr said: "Was he?"

"Shut up, Mr. Carr!"

"I didn't buy the morning papers. We were so anxious to get away that the news didn't matter to us. No, Mr. Frisbee, we didn't know anything had happened to Mr. Daniels."

"We thought he must be in Trenton. We even talked about it," Mrs. Daniels volunteered.

"You talked about it! Gloried in your triumph!"

"I object," from Mr. Black.

"All right. That's your story. You didn't know about the murder—until when?"

"We read about it in the Chicago papers. Then a detective, Pearlman, met me in the lobby, and, without knowing he was actually looking for me, he told me about it."

"And you, Mr. Chandler. Did you notice anything strange about your undertaking parlor when you arrived the morning of October fourth?"

"I noticed there was no one in attendance and that the safe had been cleaned out."

"Anything else?"

"I'd like to talk this matter over with my attorney before I answer that question."

"Granted. Go ahead. There's a little room right there."

As the two men rose: "How long will it take you?"

"I don't know."

"Please make it as quickly as possible."

"Yes, sir."

The door closed behind them.

2
FAMILIAR SOUNDS

THE next-door neighbor of the Daniels family in Trenton, George Olmstead, was tuning in on the radio as his wife washed the dinner dishes. Suddenly, there was the sound of a garage door opening. So intent was he upon getting the correct wave length that a motor had started and tires had begun to crunch the gravel drive before he realized that he was hearing once more familiar sounds for the first time in many weeks.

His wife with a dripping platter in her hand stood in the doorway, listening.

"That's next door."

"Yeah, somebody's driving the Daniels' car out of the garage."

"You better see who it is."

"Not me. I don't want to get mixed up in that mess!"

"George! Somebody may be stealing it."

"Let 'em steal. Y'think I want my head blown off just to find out?"

Mrs. Olmstead was less timid. She looked out the front window as the car gained the street, backing, then turned and drove rapidly away.

"It's a man, George."

"Well?"

"You ought to call the police."

"I'm not going to call the police. I've had all the trouble I want with that outfit. If you want to call the police, go ahead."

"I don't care anything about it one way or the other, but that man certainly drove that car out of there as if he had done it before."

"You think it was Daniels?"

"I couldn't see his face."

"I heard to-day that he wasn't dead, that they cooked that story up so they could collect the insurance."

"But two strange men found him on the street."

"Yeah, but according to to-night's paper, it wasn't him."

3
WARNING

RAYMOND called Sybil on the phone and asked:

"Has any one called me, Sybil?"

"Oh, Mr. Fitzgerald. There's two detectives here asking for you. They're going to arrest you. They've searched the house, and they are waiting out in front this very minute."

"What are they going to arrest me for?"

"They say you've got Richard Roe and Tommy Freeman both hid somewhere and that you're interfering with the law."

"They did?"

"They're out in front o' the house this minute an' they told me if I warned you they'd take me along, too."

"Call them to the phone, Sybil."

"Oh, no, Mr. Raymond. Mrs. Horn won't even let 'em back in the house."

"You just call them to the phone, Sybil. I'll fix it with Mrs. Horn when I get home."

"Should I, really?"

"Sure, go ahead. That's a good girl. I'll hold the wire."

"All right. You hold the wire."

Wanted to arrest him! What next?

A gruff voice said: "Hello."

"Hello, Brubacher?"

"No, this is Apfel."

"Well, this is Ray Fitzgerald. Is there anything I can do for you?"

"The heck it is. Did this girl tell you what we wanted?"

"That young lady said you inquired for me."

"Yeah? Well, the chief wants to see you."

"Do you know what he wants?"

"He wants to ask you some questions."

"I see. All right, Mr. Apfel, I'll look in on him."

"You will?"

"Certainly."

"Well, that's fine, Fitzgerald. Then we won't wait for you."

"No. You go ahead an' play pool. I'll go over and see the chief myself."

But Ray left the vicinity of the telephone booth as quickly as possible. He walked to the corner of Forty-fifth Street and Fifth Avenue and started slowly in the direction of the Bond Building.

Two men had found a body at about this time of night. One man had been short, about thirty; had worn a short, yellow mustache. The other, a little taller, about the same age, smooth shaven; had a small blue pit on one side of his chin. They had walked along this walk in exactly this way. Two specific men out of all the millions of people who were in New York in the course of a year. Who were they? Where were they now?

Why had they found that body and not the two men ahead of them—or those directly behind? Why had they not corrected the police in the matter of the condition of the body? Afraid. Or had its face been hacked by an edged instrument, like a dull hatchet?

They had walked exactly like this. A gust of wind gave Ray's thoughts a push in the right direction. One of them had stepped in this doorway exactly like this, to light a cigarette out of the wind. The match had revealed the body. They had picked it up and carried it across the street, exactly like this.

The night light burned in the rich-toned interior of the undertaking parlor. No one was in sight. Ray tried the handle of the door, noiselessly. It gave slightly and would have opened if he had continued to press. But Tommy had had it locked? Why? After all, what guaranty had he that the boy had been telling him the truth? How much of Tommy's "confession" to him had been the inflamed imagination of a boy? How much fact?

They had taken the body to the rear of the place and put in on a table. They had left quickly, informed the policeman, and disappeared. Who were they? What sort of men would be walking? All sorts. Apparently, there was no way to separate those two men from any other two in the world. They might have been going to a movie, to see their sweethearts, to their place of employment. They might be upon any conceivable errand—or possibly no errand at all.

"I guess I must be a punk detective. How the devil would they go about finding two fellows like that?"

The answer, obviously, was that the paid detectives had no more notion than Ray how to go about finding those two men. If they had, they would have found them.

Ray walked as far as Broadway, then returned to Fifth Avenue, and again paced out the course the men were known to have taken. They might have entered the street from any of these buildings, then walked along here like this—to this doorway.

The young fellow leaned against the corner of the building, four feet from the place the body must have been found. A four-door sedan drew to the curb. Its driver leaned out. "Have you a got a match, young fellow?"

"Sure." Ray crossed the walk to the car, holding out a package of matches.

"Thanks. Your name Fitzgerald?"

Ray remembered that the police wanted him. "It might be."

"I guess it is."

"Well?"

"Well, this: Let this Daniels case alone and go back to your job in the movies. You're not a detective and you're wasting your time."

"Who are you?"

From somewhere, a strong arm brought a hard, round object against Raymond's head. He stumbled and pitched against the side of the car, senseless. The driver roughly pushed him to the walk, then drove rapidly away.

CHAPTER FIFTEEN

1
THE CORPUS DELICTI?

AS the door shut behind Joseph Chandler and Mr. Blanchard, Frisbee rose and opened the hall door. A deputy saluted. Frisbee nodded and returned to his desk. "We will have to wait for them. Come here, Zach."

Brubacher moved close to the district attorney's desk.

"What do you make of it, Zach?"

Brubacher shook his head. "You'll have to get this guy Chandler before the grand jury to make him talk. He knows more about the murder than anybody here."

Frisbee lowered his voice. "Then you don't think these two had anything to do with it?"

"Not a thing."

"And you think Daniels is in the Macnaughton vault?"

"Sure. They just got the bodies switched."

"Who—'they'?"

"The ambulance surgeons."

"They say there was only one body in the place when they got there."

"Yeah."

"But Chandler buried somebody."

"He buried something. Even the papers carried the story how Macnaughton couldn't be seen, he was so chopped up."

"You mean he might o' filled the coffin with rocks or something else like that?"

"What was to stop 'im?"

"If there's no body in the second coffin, it'll strengthen the insurance company's case."

"Right."

"Oh, Mr. Carr."

"Yes, sir."

"What's being done about opening the Macnaughton vault?"

"Mrs. Macnaughton has left town. Her lawyer is being asked for permission."

"I don't know if we dare open it without her permission."

"I guess we'll find some way around that. Her lawyer can give us the O. K."

"He can, but will he?"

"I think so. We have a man there now."

"Well, I don't know where we stand on a thing of that kind. We may have to wait."

Frisbee turned to Mrs. Daniels. "Have you any photographs of your husband, Mrs. Daniels?"

"There are quite a few in Trenton."

"Call the chief over there, Zach, and see if they've picked 'em up."

The door opened, and two scowling, serious-visaged men returned.

"Well, sir?"

"We've decided not to talk at this time, Mr. State's Attorney. If you will set a time to-morrow or the day after, we will come prepared to answer your questions. To-day it is impossible."

"Why is it impossible? If Mr. Chandler needs legal advice before aiding in any inquiry of this kind, I will wash my hands of the whole matter and let the law take its official course."

"What would that be?"

"I'll have the case reopened or I'll turn it over to the grand jury and hold every one for testimony under oath."

"That, of course, is your privilege. But we are not trying to divert the course of justice. We are only asking you to allow us to verify certain information which we may be able to assemble."

"That wouldn't do, counsel. Mr. Chandler has too much to explain. If he will not talk at this time, I shall order his immediate arrest."

"On what charge?"

"Complicity and knowledge after the fact of murder."

"You'll have a hard time to prove anything, Mr. Frisbee."

"We have an eyewitness of his attempt to destroy important evidence."

"What evidence?"

"The suit of clothes Frank Daniels wore from his home on October third; a gold, hunting-case watch belonging to the deceased, and seven hundred and fifty dollars in cash, paid to Mr. Daniels by an associate named Epstein."

"That's a lie!" Chandler shouted. "I never saw those objects."

"No? I am no longer interested in anything you have to say, Mr. Chandler. I will have to listen to it all again, probably before a jury. As you leave the building, you will be arrested. Luckily, your attorney is with you; that will make it easier for you to post your bond. Good day, sir."

Young Chandler turned to Blanchard in amazement. "Can he do that?"

"I guess he can. But don't worry about it. They can't prove a thing."

Without the courtesy of another word, the two men opened the hall door. A deputy sheriff stepped in. "All right?"

Frisbee nodded. "Let them go." When the door was closed, he turned quickly to Brubacher. "Who's with you downstairs?"

"Joe Cook."

"Tell him to shadow Chandler. We won't bother to pinch him. We'll watch him instead. And mind—get photos of Daniels from the Trenton police as quick as you can."

"Right."

"I guess the rest of you can go. We'll continue this investigation at one o'clock to-morrow afternoon. Be on time."

The deputy again questioned the right of the guests to leave. "Let them go! Come here. Don't let that man and woman out of your sight," he said, indicating Mrs. Daniels and Everett. "Take another boy with you. Stay with 'em but don't let 'em know. As soon as you get a chance, call Brubacher at the bureau, and he'll send regular dicks to take your place. Get me?"

"Sure."

"After you've called in, stay there until the relief comes and then wait to identify these two. Get me?"

"O. K."

"Beat it."

In the door, the deputy passed Brubacher returning.

"Is Cook with him?" Frisbee asked.

"Yep, but he had to take your car."

"The hell he did. Get it back. You think, I'm gonna walk home?"

"I'll have it back in half an hour." He picked up the telephone. "The bureau, Beulah."

"Tell 'em to pinch Richard Roe. We need him."

"Try to find him! Hello, the chief. Brubacher talkin'. You won't find that nut again? Hello, boss, Brubacher. I'm in Frisbee's office. Listen. Put two men in a car and shoot 'em out to Miss Weismuller's on the Drive. Joe Cook is on his way out there now, trailin' Chandler. Frisbee's orders. But he's got Frisbee's car, an' he wants it. Have the boys tell Joe to come back here with the car. I'll meet him here. An' that ain't all. Keep two men on tap for a call from two county officers now making out like they are a couple of detectives. Frisbee sicked 'em onto Mrs. Daniels an' Everett to keep it covered. Got it? These hayseeds will call up later an' tell you where to send some real cops. Wait. It ain't all. Frisbee says to pinch Richard Roe. An' get some photos of Frank Daniels from the Trenton Keystoners."

Over the wire: "What the devil does Frisbee think we're runnin' down here, a standin' army? There's ten men on the case already an' near as I can find out there ain't been no murder."

"The hell there ain't been no murder!"

"Aw right! If you're so sure there's been a murder, find me the body."

2
WHAT, AGAIN?

THE Klabe Hat Store closed its doors to the public at nine every night except Saturday. October third had not been a Saturday. Neither was this day in early December. John Peterson and Francis Kelly, both salesmen in the Klabe establishment on Forty-fifth Street, almost always left the store together. They walked toward Broadway on Forty-fifth Street. As they neared the freight entrance of the Bond Building, Peterson grabbed his companion's arm. "Let's go back."

"What's the matter?"

"There's another guy on the sidewalk."

"For God's sake!"

The street was practically deserted. One couple walked slowly on the opposite side of the street.

Ray was coming to. He raised one arm and rubbed his bursting head.

"*He* ain't dead."

"This street ain't healthy."

"Wait a minute."

Ray rolled over.

"Come on, let's get out o' this. We almost got in dutch before."

"But we can't leave a guy that's alive."

"He's drunk."

"No, he ain't."

Ray pulled himself to one knee and again rubbed his head.

"He's been hurt."

Francis Kelly ran to Fitzgerald's side and helped him to his feet. His shorter and more timid companion reluctantly followed.

"What's the matter, fellow?"

"Whew! I got—a crack—on the head."

"Held up?"

"No-no. I don't think so. Gosh, it hurts."

The young man's head was clearing, and, in the dim light from a street lamp, he scrutinized the man supporting him. On the left side of his chin, there was a small blue pit. Ray looked quickly at the other man. He had a short, well-trimmed, yellow mustache.

"Say, if you fellows'll give me a hand to the nearest speakeasy. I'll buy a drink."

3
IS DANIELS DEAD?

Two of Trenton's finest approached the door of the Daniel's home.

"The garage is open."

"The devil it is."

"So it is! An' the car's gone."

"Let's look."

Mrs. George Olmstead came to her own back porch and told the two officers what had occurred the night before.

"We didn't investigate because, after all, it was none of our business and we didn't want to be mixed up in any murder trial."

"You say he backed out of here? Must have been used to it."

"He drove the car as easily as Mr. Daniels ever did. I'll just tell you, Mr. Olmstead and I don't think he's dead at all."

"The lock's not broken. Whoever opened it had a key."

"That bird ain't dead at all. But if they're after the insurance, they'll never get it this way. It's a dead give-away."

"Say. I wonder if that bird without a memory could be Daniels? He's got away, you know."

"Maybe that's what they want the pictures for."

"Let's go! Thanks, lady."

"Don't mention it."

"Do you suppose he could?"

"I ain't got no idea. Anything is liable to happen in this squirrely case. Lord, wouldn't you think his wife'd recognize 'im if she saw his picture or somethin'?"

"Where'd she see his picture? This Richard Roe got out on bond before the newspapers got to him, an' then he jumped his bond."

"I wouldn't even bet with you."

CHAPTER SIXTEEN

1
A CALL FOR HELP

ROE was having lots of trouble. It had continued for hours. Now they were threatening to call a cop. Finally, through the mist that shrouded his brain, came recollection of a friend. If he was ever in trouble, Sybil would get him out of it, and he had her telephone number in his pocket.

He called Sybil.

"This is Richard Roe, Sybil. And I want to come over to you, and they won't let me."

"Where are you?"

"I'm in Jersey, and they won't let me on the ferries because I haven't got any money. Every time I drive up to the toll gate, they get sore and chase me away. I've been to seven different ones. I've been driving all day long thinking one of them would trust me. They all think I'm drunk, Sybil."

"Driving? What are you driving?"

"I'm driving a car, of course. You think I haven't got anything?"

"Whose car have you got?"

"I got my own car, Sybil. It's my own car. But they won't let me on the ferry because I only had ten cents."

"Where did you get a car, Richard?"

"I've always had a car, Sybil. You don't think I stole it, do you?"

"Where are you now?"

"I'm a block from the Hoboken ferry, but they won't let me on it."

"You better come over without your car, Richard. Have you got four cents?"

"Not now. It costs a dime to talk to you. I haven't got any more."

"Will you wait right there until I come to you?"

"Yes, sure I will, I'll just drive around until you get here."

"Don't you dare drive around. You just stay right where you are. What is the street address?"

"I don't know, Sybil."

"Well, *find out, quick!*"

"Just a minute. Gee, don't yell at me, Sybil!

I've had enough trouble, to-day."

"Hurry, Richard. They'll cut you off for overtime unless you hurry."

"Well, I am hurrying. Gee whiz!"

"Hello."

"Hello."

"It's 209 Beech Street, Hoboken. Will you come over and get me?"

"Right away. For Heaven's sake, don't move from there."

"No, I won't. I'll wait. Good-by, Sybil."

"Good-by!"

2
HOME AGAIN

THAT night, Tommy tried to get into his home. He wanted to see his mother. He was sick. He was tired. He was afraid. The only congenial soul he had met since October third, the only man he thought he could trust, had betrayed him into strange and hostile hands. Now the city had beaten him. Its noises had bruised his brain. Sight of a policeman's uniform was like a spur to the raw side of an exhausted horse. If his eyes met those of a smooth-shaven adult in a fedora, he blanched and hastened on, lest it be a plainclothes man.

He wanted his mother and the comforting aura of safety that enveloped her and the shabby East Side home.

He stood for a long time at the corner, watching his house. Two blocks away, an elevated train passed, then another. He would wait until the next train went by. Then, if nothing had happened, if he saw nothing suspicious, he would walk slowly to the door, as if there were no reason for hurrying—as if he lived upstairs, or something.

Two detectives passed him without arousing his easily started fear. They walked to the middle of the block and separated.

"That's the kid."

"You sure?"

"Pretty sure. You stay here and watch the door. I'll go back on the other side and see if I can't start him."

An elevated train passed two blocks away. Tom started slowly toward his home. His step quickened. He paid no attention to the detectives. His feet were not obeying his thoughts. Faster and faster, he walked until he began to run.

The detective stepped from the shadow, and the boy sped past without pausing or even looking at the house. Around the corner and to the next. Faster and faster, he ran, the two big men in pursuit. He left them far behind. He realized they were chasing him. He circled the entire block and was in the familiar hall before they had fully determnied which turn he had taken.

"Ma! Oh, ma!" He pounded on the door. "Ma, let me in quick. Ma, for God's sake, if anybody comes tell 'em I ain't here. Say you ain't seen me at all."

"My boy!"

3
A LITTLE FUN

Two inconspicuous arms of the law studied the register of the Majestic Arms Hotel.

"They got separate rooms."

"They got troubles enough without tryin' to get away with a Saturday night 'Mr. and Mrs.' Of course, they got separate rooms."

"Have these two rooms got a connectin' bath?"

The room clerk investigated. "Yes, sir."

"Well, you can't blame 'em for that either. She's a very good-lookin' woman."

Directly over the detectives' heads, fourteen floors above them, Mrs. Daniels turned from her mirror to Everett. "Charley."

"Yes?"

"Would it seem too awful if we went to a show to-night? I'm so tired of thinking about nothing but this—this terrible affair."

"It wouldn't seem awful at all. Of course, we'll go. We'll see a musical comedy."

"You're such a darling."

"I'll get a paper, and we'll pick one out."

The telephone operator had just received her instructions to record carefully and to report every call from the two rooms.

She told the detectives: "*He* called from *her* room for an evening paper."

"Connectin' bath is a good idea."

Their own names leered at them from the front page of the newspaper. Charley quickly found the theatrical page and threw the balance of the evening news in the wastebasket.

"Oh, how will it end! I'm so tired of it. So very tired of it."

"Everything will be all right, dear. They haven't anything against us that they can prove."

"No, they can't prove anything. But it's torture to answer their questions. It's horrible to have them thinking we are murderers."

"And thieves."

"Poor boy!"

"Oh, that hurts, Bea. That hurts to have the young man think I stole his money. After all the years I worked for his father."

"Oh! Let's forget it."

"Do you think the 'Frolics' would be good?"

"I doubt if we could get in. We can try."

"At a scalper's?"

"I think they have a ticket service here in the hotel."

The telephone girl reported that two tickets had been secured for the "Frolics."

"Give us one seat on each side of those two if you have to rebuild the theater.

"Say, this case ain't so bad. I ain't seen a good show in months."

"They tell me the 'Frolics' are terrible."

"I heard it was good."

"Well, we're seein' it, good or bad."

4
BY WIRELESS

To the Macnaughton yacht, ambling slowly back from Bimini, came a wireless of prodigious length.

Would Mrs. Macnaughton return at once to New York? The police had found some reason to wish to open the family vault in Glenn View. In their search for the murderer of a Trenton hardware merchant, they had exhumed a body in Trenton which had been identified by an undertaker *and her own doctor* as that of her late husband. Could she return to New York at once to testify before the grand jury at the urgent request of Assistant District Attorney Frisbee? Had he—her late husband's partner—done right in giving the police permission to open the vault? He was much distressed to be the cause of so much annoyance. He was sorry to be forced to bring the matter to her attention at all. Only the demands of the police department searching for a criminal still at large and entirely unknown had forced him to wireless.

Mrs. Macnaughton answered immediately.

Rushing home at once. Extend police every courtesy. Cannot understand situation. Suggest you communicate at once with young Mr. Joseph Chandler, the undertaker. I knew his father well.

Mrs. Clark C. Macnaughton.

5
THE SEETHING FRISBEE

THE papers ran as follows:

UNSEAL MACNAUGHTON VAULT

———

FRISBEE TAKES DRASTIC ACTION
IN SEARCH FOR DANIELS' BODY

———

The fifty-thousand-dollar mausoleum of Clark C. Macnaughton will be opened by the police to-morrow in an effort to find the body of Frank Daniels. It was the opinion of the police to-day that the bodies of the illustrious corporation counsel, Charles C. Macnaughton, and the wealthy hardware merchant of Trenton had in some unaccountable manner been transposed before burial.

The office of Assistant District Attorney Frisbee seethed with internal conflict to-day when the scandalous suggestion of incompetence and gross neglect of duty was made regarding several city departments.

The finger of accusation pointed in various directions, but no charges were made public. Mr. Frisbee said: "Until we open the Macnaughton vault, I have nothing to say. But, believe me, I am going to shake this whole town apart to find out just what happened last October third and fourth."

6
ON A RAMPAGE

FRISBEE paced the floor of his office, screaming his disgust, demanding to know of an Omnipotent Providence why he made men without giving them brains.

Officer Barnes and three men in the white uniforms of ambulance attendants sulked in chairs before him.

"Why didn't you look at the body, you half-wit?"

"Now listen, Mr. Frisbee, you're a long ways up over me, and I'm only a common copper, but I ain't no half-wit and the looey himself told me at the fire that I'd done my duty an' I should leave the body to the medical examiner."

"The medical examiner! Where is that num-skull?" Frisbee jerked the receiver from the hook. "Beulah! Where is Evansborough? Didn't I tell you to have him here in my office?"

"He doesn't answer, Mr. Frisbee. I've been calling him ever since. He didn't report for duty yesterday, and no one knows where he is."

"Give me the bureau. Now some one is tampering with the examiner. Carr most likely. I'll shake this whole town apart 'til I find out what——Hello, chief! This is Frisbee. Yes, Frisbee. One of the city's prize doctors is missin', and I want him. Doc Evansborough that turned in this report on the so-called Daniels body ain't been seen in a week. Find him an' bring him here."

"You want the whole detective bureau put on one case? You got twenty men on that comedy murder already. I ain't got nobody to send."

"Now, listen, chief. As a personal favor to me, find out where this doctor is. I've got to talk to him, an' I think somebody has got to him ahead o' me."

From the phone, he turned on the three internes, sneering. "And you prize dumb-bells walk into a morgue an' take the first stiff you come to whether you have any right to it or not."

"It was the only body in the place, Mr. Frisbee. We looked."

"Why didn't you call back an' say there wasn't anybody in attendance?"

"We reported that as soon as we got back."

"It don't appear on the record."

"Well, I told Si."

"Si? What did you tell Si for? Why didn't you write it down? Did you ever read the instruction book? How long you been on an ambulance?"

"Three months."

"An' you were in charge?"

"Yes, sir."

"Didn't they have anybody with brains at the morgue?"

Another interne came to his partner's defense. "We got a call to pick up a body at Chandler. We go an' pick up the only body we saw. His clothes was on the table right there. I don't see nothin' so dumb in that."

"It was dumb enough to cost you your job. Get out—all of you! Go back to work! I'll call you when I need you again."

CHAPTER SEVENTEEN

1
THE KID FROM STAMFORD

THE chief of detectives looked up from the *Racing Form.* "Well, thank goodness, you're back. Go down an' see who busted into the cashier's cage at the Hunt Furniture Factory to the tune of twenty thousand bucks: This is a devil of a detective bureau—one detective."

"This is the kid from Stamford."

"I know who he is, an' we'll try to make 'im happy. Go on down to the furniture factory an' find out what happened."

"Yes, sir. Shall I leave the kid here?"

"Yes, leave 'im here. An' forget this Daniels case. I got four more calls for you to make before night.

"Frisbee's got an idea that New York quits committin' crime just because he's got a murder to work on.

"Well, young fellow, are you the boy that found all that money?"

"Yes, sir, and the watch."

"You ready to tell the folks all about it?"

"Yes, sir."

"Could you identify the man you saw that day if you should ever see him again?"

"I think so. Yes, sir."

"Aw right. You come along with me, an' we'll have the sheriff get you a place to stay while you're here."

"Yes, sir."

2
THE STONE WALL WEAKENS

OLD Robert Daniels stalked with his cane to the rear of the hardware store. "Phillips, they tell me you saw Frank the other day. That true?"

"Yes, sir, Mr. Daniels, it is. He came up here to the window and looked in and stood there for a minute. At first, I thought my eyes were playing me tricks, but I'm convinced they weren't because, as I came toward the front of the store, he turned and took off up the street like all get out."

"And you're sure it was Frank?"

"I'm positive."

"I'm glad."

Phillips almost fainted. In three years, he had never heard this old millionaire speak a kind word for his nephew. The shock was almost too much.

"You're—glad?"

"I'm glad if it's true. I didn't like to think of him dead. After all, I been pretty hard on him."

"That—that's—er—your business of course. Mr. Daniels always treated me all right."

"Of course, he did. He was a fine man. But if he ain't dead, Phillips, what's the matter with him?"

"The papers are all saying it was a plot to get his insurance."

"Phillips, there's something fishy about this whole business, and I mean to find out what it is. Will you help me?"

"Why, yes, sir. I'll do anything on earth I can."

"All right, then. You do this. Just keep a very close watch around the store here—and move over into his house to sleep. Live there. And keep your eyes open. Some one's taken his car out of the garage. First thing we know they'll start tearing the place down. Will you do it?"

"Why certainly, sir. When shall I move in?"

"I wish you would go over there to-night. Somehow, I think we will learn more that way. I don't know why."

3
MORE DIRTY WORK

BUT no one was watching Mr. Carr. While Mrs. Daniels and Everett sat between two operatives in a theater; while two more detectives drove furiously to keep pace with Chandler and his sweetheart; while two others panted after Tommy Freeman and two others, lounging before Ray Fitzgerald's rooming house, saw Sybil run out and hail a passing cab—while all of these and several more employees of the city and State watched and waited and chased, no one bothered Mr. Carr. His way led to a tough speakeasy on the lower East Side where a Russian wench of mountainous proportions dispensed rotgut at twenty-five cents a drink.

The sole customer regarded the young lawyer askance from a filthy table against the wall.

"I'm looking for a man named Petrov," he told the colossal woman.

"Yeah? I dunno."

"You know Petrov."

"Three-four Petrov."

"Aleck? Aleck Petrov?"

"I dunno."

"He comes here."

"I dunno."

Carr laid a five-dollar bill on the bar.

"I don't want to know where he lives. I only want to see him. Can you get him to come here later on to-night?"

The woman looked longingly at the money, then shook her head. "No. I dunno."

The other customer came to the bar. "For me?"—indicating the money. "I take you?"

"Sure. You know him?"

"Sure. Alexis." He took the bill. "I show you."

Carr followed the man to the street.

"Is it far?"

"He's on a ship."

"Fine."

The blackness of the docks swallowed them.

4
PERFECT ACTING

THEN Tommy's mother put Duse and Bernhardt to shame. She answered the knock of the breathless detectives.

"We'll have to search your house, Mrs. Freeman. We saw your boy come in here."

"You saw my Tommy? Where is he? Did he come in here?"

"Never mind stalling. You just let us look around."

"You can look. Of course, you can look. But if he came in, he must have gone on upstairs, and I'm going to see." She passed them quickly and began a rheumatic ascent of the front stairs.

"You better follow 'er. I'll go through the house."

One man followed the old lady to the second floor, the third, the fourth. The other opened doors cautiously and peered under the beds and into the closets. In fifteen minutes, they were both on the street.

"I don't think he'd come back here. He was too scared."

"We lost him on the second corner. His mother ain't seen him."

"He's still runnin'."

"Yeah. He won't try to get in again for a week."

"Let's eat."

"One of us ought to wait."

"Aw, no. That kid ain't got nerve enough to come back to-night. We'll tap the telephone after we eat an' see what happens." They walked to a lunch room and sat where they could watch the street.

A taxi drew to the curb close to the Freeman home, and Ray Fitzgerald got out. He mounted the steps and, from the stoop, surveyed the street. Satisfied that he was not watched, he darted quickly into the Freeman hall. His knock aroused a whispered consultation, then the boy's mother suddenly opened the door.

"Raymond!"

"Hello, Mrs. Freeman." The door closed. "Have you heard from Tommy?"

She did not answer but stood looking deep into his eyes, attempting to find duplicity there.

"Is he here?"

"No-o."

"He is! Oh, Mrs. Freeman, please trust me. Please get Tommy to trust me. I'm getting at the bottom of this thing at last, and I've got to have his help. Is he here?"

The old lady's intuition was stronger than her sense of honor. She had promised Tommy she would betray him to no one, but she could not doubt Ray's sincerity. "Tommy," she called. "Tommy. Come on out, son. It's Raymond, and he wants to help you."

5
ANOTHER ESCAPE

TAKING advantage of their prerogative as legal pursuers, the two men on the trail of Chandler and Miss Weismuller ran through the traffic lights at the wrong corner. A touring car lurched into them, tearing and rending. There were no casualties, but the quarry escaped.

"I don't care what you've done, Joe. I love you," June whispered. "Let's go ahead. Let's drive somewhere and get married to-night."

"There's been an accident back of us."

"Shall we stop?"

"I don't know what we could do. Some fool tried to beat the lights."

"Don't you want to, Joe?"

"I want to, darling. But we can't get a license until morning. And how upset every one will be—running off that way."

"Isn't it better? After all, if this trouble is going to mean a lot of nasty publicity——"

"It may mean more than nasty publicity. Suppose they put me in the penitentiary?"

"They can't! Surely, you are not to blame."

"But my silence has caused the police a lot of trouble. That suit of clothes—and everything. Oh, I was mad to do what I did. If I had only felt in the lining."

"What does Blanchard say?"

"He's at home now trying to find some law that covers it. When I told him the truth, he just shook his head and said he had never heard or read of anything like it."

"Does he think they can put you—in the penitentiary for that?"

"He will be up all night trying to find out. Oh, thank goodness, I'm out of that ghastly business."

"But, Joe, what do you think really happened? Just what is your own theory?"

"Oh, I haven't any clear idea. This fellow had been killed by a mighty blow on the side of his head. His neck was broken, his jaw splintered. I imagined he had been held up, but, if all that money was in the lining of his clothes—probably that's wrong."

"You don't suspect his wife and Mr. Everett?"

"No-o-o. I think they were just eloping. I don't believe they had him killed."

"Have you ever seen this man who doesn't know who he is?"

"That's a dodge, June. He's as sane as any one. I've never seen him. I don't know what he has to do with the affair. But I don't believe he's crazy."

"Let's get something cool to drink."

"All right."

CHAPTER EIGHTEEN

1
PINCH THE CONTENTS

AS Sybil left her home to meet Richard Roe, the detectives watching the house followed her unattractive figure with their eyes.

"Now where is that moll flyin' to?"

"That guy's called her."

"We ought to tap the phone. Who d'you mean?"

"Either one of 'em. Prob'ly Fitzgerald."

"Y'think we ought t'follow 'er?"

"Prob'ly it's a blind to lead us away from here so he can get in."

"We better sit tight."

"Yeah. We ain't got no orders to trail her."

"She's near as crazy as Roe, that one."

"She's worse. She reminds me of a moll I had to trail when I was workin' for Burns. Ugly as sin but a stepper. Her old man thought she was loose an' he had 'er shadowed. What a time I had!"

Hours passed.

"Let's eat. There's no sense waitin' around here all night. He knows we're here. He ain't comin' home."

"That car's been there for a devil of a time."

"Where?"

"That one."

"Looks like that kid on the *Record's* car."

"It is."

"What's that?"

In the seat of Jake's roadster sat the trussed and gagged figure of a dock laborer, his black eyes spitting fire.

"Well, fellow, who's been playin' Halloween jokes on you?"

"Take the gag out o' his mouth."

"Who are you?"

"I didn't do nothin'. I work hard. I didn't do nothin'."

"Bill, meet an honest guy at last. He works hard, but he don't do nothin'."

"Who tied you up?"

"Two men. I don't know who they are."

"How long you been here?"

"Long time. Two hours."

"You been settin' here two hours?"

"An' we never saw 'im?"

"Who brought you here?"

"One man. He tie me up. Other man stand and watch. Two hours. Then they put me in here and bring me here. I been here two hours."

"Where'd you get tied up?"

"In the Bronx."

"That's a good place."

"An' you don't know who did it?"

"No."

"What'd they tie you for?"

"I dunno."

"They steal anything?"

"No."

"What d'you make o' that?"

"Come here."

They moved to the wall of the building.

"That's young Jacob's car. He's a friend of Fitzgerald. There's somethin' in this,"

"Let's get ahold of Jake."

"You go call him. I'll talk to this bird."

"What's your name?"

"Matty?"

"Matty what?"

"Matty Benowski."

"Where do you live, Matty?"

"On Putnam Street."

"Where do you work?"

"I'm stevedore. McManus Dock Corporation."

"What were you doin' in the Bronx?"

"I was look for a man."

"What man?"

"Man tell me he got job paintin' houses. I come there he give me more money."

"What's his name?"

"His name Bill."

"Bill what?"

"I donno."

"Where does he live?"

"I donno."

"How were you gonna find him?"

"I lost address. He gave me on a little slip paper. I lost him. You gonna take off these tie?"

"I guess so."

As the detective finished untying the hand-kerchiefs, cravats and rags, with which the man had been crudely but securely bound, his partner returned.

"Jake ain't there, but he left word at the city desk that if the law found his car to just leave it where it was but to pinch the contents. He must of known this guy was in it."

"Did you steal this car?"

"How could he steal it?"

"That's right. Said to pinch the contents, eh?"

"Yeah. I'll bet this is more Daniels business. Let's send this guy in."

Thirty minutes later Matty was in a cell.

CHAPTER NINETEEN

1
AT THE VAULT

A PROCESSION of ten or more quiet figures in single file crunched the gravel path that led to the Macnaughton vault. The vice president of the Glenn View Cemetery, Incorporated, turned to the nearest policeman. "The front gate of the cemetery was broken open last night while the watchman was eating his lunch after midnight. So far, we haven't missed anything."

"Man'd be a fool to break into a cemetery. Seems to me they'd be anxious enough to stay out."

The procession halted, and the partner of the late Clark C. Macnaughton advanced with the sexton to the vault door.

"Well, look at that!"

"It's been broken open!"

"Mr. Brubacher," Frisbee raised his voice, "you'd better take charge here. Some one has opened this vault!"

Brubacher strode to the front of the line. "Broke in, huh?"

"They chiseled the lock."

Brubacher waved the group back. "Everybody stay on the walks. I'll have to look for footprints later. Everybody stay back there on the walks."

Frisbee bustled officiously forward and back. "Who broke that open, anyway?"

Brubacher cocked one eye at his superior. "Better pinch Chandler for something or other. Ten to one, he did this."

Frisbee whispered to his aid: "Stay at Chandler's elbow. If he insists on leaving, arrest him."

"Yes, sir."

"Well, Mr. Brubacher, you are in charge. Tell us what to do. Are you going in?"

"Ahem! Of course, I am," he said, pulling on his gloves. "We'll have to take finger prints."

"Can I take a shot at the gate before you open it, Mr. Brubacher?" A tabloid reporter pushed his camera forward. "Thank you."

Brubacher pushed the iron gate back and stepped into the gloomy vault. An inner door had also been chiseled open. It stood ajar. An ambitious cameraman exploded a flash light, without waiting for permission. The detective swung that door, gingerly, taking care not to disturb any possible finger prints.

"You'll all have to stay outside. There may be footprints in here."

Heedless of his words, the reporters pushed on. Several policemen pulled them back and stood in the outer door of the mausoleum.

Frisbee walked to Chandler's side: "Do you know anything about this, Mr. Chandler?"

"I do not."

"Who else would want to get into this vault?"

"Why should *I* want to get into it?"

"You know very well."

"I have no idea what you're talking about."

"Do you know anything about this, Mrs. Daniels?"

"No, sir."

"Do you?"—turning to Everett.

"No, sir."

"Do you, Mr. Carr?"

"I do not."

"Any of you know anything about this?"

There was a general shaking of heads.

"We noticed the front gate early this morning——" the vice president began.

Brubacher had found the coffins. There were three, all, seemingly, of ancient date. He returned to the door. "Mr. Chandler, will you come here, please? Walk very carefully, on your heels."

"Were you in here the day of the funeral?"

"Certainly."

"How many coffins were there?"

"Three."

"You put in the fourth?"

"Yes."

"Is the one you put in here now?"

"No."

"Where is it?"

"I do not know."

They returned to the waiting group. "You'll have to stay here, officer. We can't leave this place unguarded."

"Yes, sir."

"Stay here until you are relieved if it takes all night."

"Yes, sir."

"You can do anything you want to with these guests o' yours, Frisbee. I'll be busy here for an hour."

"Come along. We'll go back to my office."

They filled three cars, each of the supposedly free men and women escorted by an armed member of the department for law enforcement.

Frisbee turned to Carr and asked: "Now what do you make of that? There's more nonsense connected with this case than any I ever saw before. There are agents at liberty working against us. Say, that was a break for you. Suppose Daniels was in that coffin. You'd be in a hole."

"Sure I would, but you don't think——"

"I never think. It is not becoming to an assistant district attorney."

"Well, you needn't be suspicious of me. I'll admit that I take a long shot now and then, but I haven't gone in for grave robbing."

"It'll go hard with whoever did it, and I'll find out who it was if it takes a year."

2
BRUBACHER SCORES

BRUBACHER watched the cars drive away, taking, he reasoned, the only people known who could benefit by this rifling of the Macnaughton tomb. There were Mrs. Daniels and Everett. If they had killed Daniels or had him killed, they would not want the body found. It had disappeared once, aiding the murderer, whoever he was. Now it was gone again.

Suppose the coffin had not contained Daniels' body. Chandler would benefit. He would save his face. He would never want it revealed that he had filled a coffin with stones— a coffin that should have contained the body of an illustrious man. It would hurt his business, ruin his reputation. But he had sold out. He need not care if the truth were known. Suppose that coffin contained a body other than Frank Daniels. Suppose it contained the body of the boy who had been in the undertaker's that night, Tommy Freeman. Would Chandler, in a rage at finding the Macnaughton body missing,

have struck the young assistant—perhaps killed him acciden-
tally, and then buried him instead of Macnaughton? Or, if the
boy was gone, would he have struck down another man, to fill
that expensive coffin?

Chandler had entered the parlors in the morning. His
big funeral was scheduled for ten-thirty, He had two hours
and a half—and the body was missing. Could he get a less
distinguished body from one of his other shops? Would he
commit murder to avoid confessing that he had *lost* Clark C.
Macnaughton's remains? At that time, he had no idea that
Daniels or any other dead man had been brought to that parlor,
the night before.

The first knowledge he had of a body being taken from his
morgue by the police had been hours after he had buried—whatever it was he buried. No, the idea was preposterous. Chandler
was no murderer. He had found Daniels' body somewhere in his
establishment where the ambulance men had overlooked it. He
had buried it in Macnaughton's place—knowingly or unknow-
ingly. But he must have known it was not Macnaughton or he
would not have attempted to destroy that suit of clothes. But suppose some one else had taken his car for that purpose. The boy
from Stamford had not identified him yet. All that was certain
was his ownership of the car—and the fact that he had dismissed
the chauffeur two hours before.

Without a doubt, the missing coffin contained the body
of Frank Daniels and only the murderer—and the Atlantic
Insurance Company—could benefit by destroying that body.
The murderer and the insurance company! Then, no matter what
Chandler knew, no matter what he had done, unless he was actually the man who killed Frank Daniels, he had not stolen the
body. The day was past when the contents of that coffin could
have worked him any real damage.

It had been the murderer. Whoever he was, he was still at large. Brubacher could do no more than collect what clues remained about the cemetery.

Or it had been Carr, the attorney for the insurance company. The actions of Mrs. Daniels and Everett the night before had been accounted for minutely by the detectives set to watch them. Who had *not* been watched? Carr had not been watched. Richard Roe was still running loose. Tommy Freeman had never been caught. And who was the fellow found in the parked auto before Roe's rooming house?

If it were not for Chandler's eight thousand missing dollars——

Brubacher scrutinized the marks of the chisel. A common inch and a quarter chisel had been used, one with a nick on it not far from the center. Tracks established that a light truck of common make with well-worn tires had been used to carry the coffin away. These marks in the turf, revealing how the truck had stood, how turned, started the detective's mind in another direction.

No matter who would benefit by the deed, it was likely that hired accomplices had assisted in the actual performance, if they had not carried out some one's instructions without aid. The clue he would gather here would probably lead only to hirelings. But, if they were apprehended, the source of the money might be learned. And the source of the money might be—Frank Daniels' murderer.

Three men had assisted at the grave robbing. Brubacher took measurements and records. One wall of the tomb revealed a set of five perfect finger prints.

He walked again to the gate. The same chisel had been used here. But a few feet from the gate, the fence had been scaled. Two men had climbed the fence and dropped to the grass inside.

Why should two of them climb the fence if the gate was open? He compared the footprints. The men who climbed the fence had *not* participated in the robbing of the tomb. These were distinctly different footprints from those near and in the tomb.

"How you makin' out?" asked the uniformed officer at the vault door.

"They was five men in here last night. But only three of 'em is guilty."

"Whadaya mean?"

"Two guys climbed the fence. God knows why. Then a truck drove in, after bustin' the lock on the street gate."

Brubacher returned to the fence and attempted to follow the tracks of the first men to enter the cemetery. "They must 'a' been the first in 'cause they could 'o' used the gate later."

The trail ran parallel to the main road, then switched and crisscrossed behind stone and shrubs that would have shielded the men from the road. "Uh-hum! They didn't want the three boys in the truck to see 'em. Hello!" A chisel lay at his feet. Careful to preserve any possible finger prints, Brubacher wrapped it up in a handkerchief. His brow was furrowed, for that chisel had no nicks on it, but appeared as new as if it had but that day been purchased.

Behind a monument, the two trails stopped. There the two had stood and watched the rifling of the tomb.

"Now who would that be?"

Two chisels! Could the first two men have been in the grave-yard for the same purpose? What did the man in the reporter's automobile have to do with this? A reporter would do anything to get something for his paper. Could Jacobs have been here? Was the fellow now in jail one of the grave robbers?

The officer could not disguise the respect he felt for Brubacher. "How you makin' out?" He was inquiring into the fourth dimension. He was asking God why grass was green. This man looked at the ground and walked about, silently, then spoke and what he said was true. The process was too intricate for him to follow.

"We've already got one o' these guys in jail."

"What?"

"Yep. Pinched him las' night."

"Oh, you have!"

CHAPTER TWENTY

1
CHANDLER TELLS

IN his office again, Frisbee contemplated the assemblage with hostile eyes. "Gentlemen, and Mrs. Daniels, I have gone as far with this inquiry as I possibly can. I am going to turn my evidence over to the grand jury and let them proceed as they see fit. I have gone as far as I can in the face of this opposition. When a murderer robs a tomb to cover his crime, I am unable to proceed further without every vestige of known fact regarding the case that may exist. Since you insist upon misleading me and withholding important evidence, I am forced to place you all under indictment as material witnesses.

"You, Mr. Chandler, have willfully withheld facts that must be known. For instance, you know the contents of that missing coffin. Probably no other man alive is certain of it. You and only you could *know* whether the contents of that coffin is sufficient to convict a man or woman of murder."

"That coffin contains——"

"I do not care to hear it, sir. I am, for the time being, through with this case."

"But Mr. Frisbee," Carr objected. "What are you going to indict these people for? Where is your case?"

"I'll build a case. That's none of your business."

"It may be none of my business. But it seems to me you are making a great deal of to-do about a mere disappearance. After all, this isn't a murder case."

"Not a murder case?"

"No, who is dead?"

"Mr. Frank Daniels is dead."

"Oh, is he? I have not seen the body."

"You've seen the medical examiner's verdict."

"I've seen that, yes. But we have also seen that your examiner was mistaken and that the body he examined was that of Clark C. Macnaughton. Unless you can produce the body of Frank Daniels, I do not see how you can charge any one with murder."

"The body was identified——"

"By what? By a pile of clothing and a few letters and cards. Really, Mr. Frisbee, this is scarcely identification."

"Well, we had the body once, and we'll find it again. You can't prove that the man is alive, Mr. Carr, just because his body has been stolen."

"I should shudder at the State's attempt to electrocute some one because Frank Daniels left his clothing in Mr. Chandler's undertaking parlor."

"Well, how did they get there?"

"He may have left them there when he called on Mr. Everett. I have no way of knowing. All that we actually know is that he was there, alive, at six o'clock in the evening and that at midnight his clothing was there without him."

"Mr. Frisbee, I'm ready to talk," Chandler said. "You may as well let me help you now. The coffin that was stolen from Macnaughton's vault contains the body of a man I believe to be Frank Daniels. He was killed by a blow on the head which broke his neck and his jaw bone, and possibly fractured his skull."

2
THE AMATEUR BRAGS

BRUBACHER returned to detective headquarters. As he entered the office, the chief hailed him. "C'mere! It's a long distance from Trenton. That guy Fitzgerald."

"Hello," said Brubacher.

"Hello, Brubacher?"

"Yes."

"This is Ray Fitzgerald. I'm coming in to your office just as quick as I can get there, and I'm bringing you the Daniels case in a bag."

"Yeah!"

"And if you'll tell Frisbee to hold up any definite action, it'll save him a lot of embarrassment."

"My, you talk big! Who the devil do you think you are?"

"Never mind, Brubacher. If you think I'm bluffing, watch the news stands for the home edition of the *Record*. It'll have the complete story of the murder and last night's grave robbery thrown in free. G'-by."

3
THE PRESS

THE afternoon papers with the exception of the *Record* announced in screaming type that the Macnaughton vault had been rifled the night before. The *Record* printed the details.

4
LOVERS MEET AGAIN

THE evening before, Richard Roe had obeyed Sybil. He had not moved from the place he had telephoned until the girl found him nearly an hour later.

"I thought you'd never get here."

"I came just as quick as I could."

"Have you got enough money for some gasoline? I'm nearly out."

"Richard Roe, where did you get that car?"

"That's my own car, Sybil. I own it."

"Where did you get it, Richard?"

"I got it from the garage."

"What garage?"

"My own garage."

"Take me to it!"

"To my garage? All right."

5
ALSO THE NIGHT BEFORE

"TOMMY, we're going to break another law. Are you game?"

"Anything you say, Ray. You know best."

"We've got to get a look at the body in the Macnaughton vault."

"I'm scared to death o' dead bodies now. I never used to mind."

"So am I, but I don't see any other way out. If that body is the one I think it is, our case is complete. We can go to the police and tell them the whole story."

"An' then what? I go to jail."

"No, you won't. Not the way I'll tell it."

"But they're gonna open that vault to-morrow. It's in all the papers."

"But they won't let us see it. Both of us are wanted. They'll pinch us on sight."

"They'll pinch us all the quicker for breaking into that vault. Anyway, we couldn't do it."

"Why not? Look here, Tommy. We've got to see that guy before we're pinched. Once they arrest us, we're sunk. After that, we do what they say. But if we can find out for sure that Chandler put that fellow in Macnaughton's coffin, we're all set. Then all we'll have to do is revive Richard Roe's memory, and I don't think that will be hard."

"All right, Ray. You're the boss. But I don't think we ought to do anything more. Honest, ain't I done enough?"

"Come on. I've got to see who that is."

CHAPTER TWENTY-ONE

1
GRAVE ROBBERS

THE blackest night in December shrouded the actions of the two foolhardy boys who scaled the high iron fence of the cemetery and hid swiftly behind some shrubs.

"That," whispered Ray, "is that; now if we can only find this Macnaughton vault——"

There was a rasping of metal behind them, a muffled clank and a scraping, then a screeching of heavy hinges.

"You think they've seen us?"

"Sh!"

"They're chasing us?"

"Be still."

A truck, in second, driven without lights, turned into the cemetery gate, paused for some one to board it, and continued down the graveled road.

"Come on, Tommy. Let's see what's going on."

Curves in the road allowed the two walkers to keep abreast of the truck as it penetrated to the center of the graveyard. Finally, its halting progress stopped. A flash light was turned on a vault:

MACNAUGHTON

"Tommy, we couldn't have found it without them."

"Who d'you suppose it is?"

"Well, it's not the police."

The flash light was extinguished, and the rasping of metal began again, followed once more by the creak of rusted hinges.

"Let's get over behind that monument. I want to see what's going on."

"Who do you suppose they are?"

"We'll have to get their license number as they leave. Gosh, this place gives me the creeps."

"Don't let 'em see you."

"Sh!"

"How many are there?"

"I couldn't tell. Sh!"

For a long time, no sound broke the appalling stillness. The men were inside the tomb. On the street, more than two hundred yards away, a motor passed, intensifying the immediate quiet by its soft, unreal purr. The marble and granite shafts rose in the blackness like trees in a nightmare forest.

After a wait that had become almost unbearable, the ghouls returned with the coffin between them. Ray put his lips to Tommy's ear. "Go as quiet as you can! Stay on the grass! Get a cab and have it waiting near the gate! We'll follow 'em."

"You gonna stay here?"

"Yeah. You wait in the cab—not too near the gate, so if they see the cab they won't be suspicious."

"Yeah." Tommy slipped quickly away.

The back of the truck was lowered as noiselessly as possible, and the coffin lifted in. In the blackness of the clouded night, nothing could be seen distinctly, but the silhouette of the group against the gray of the tomb showed their errand plainly.

Ray heard Tommy trip, probably on a low headstone, and crash to the ground. One of the grave robbers also heard it.

"What the devil was that?"

"What?"

"I heard som'n."

"Y'r nuts."

"Wait."

Ray held his breath.

"We can't stall like this. You're hearin' things."

"They could send us up for life for this."

"Shut up an' let's get out o' here."

"Sure."

The men climbed in the truck and it turned, slowly, as quietly as possible, and started for the gate.

Ray bounded in pursuit, leaping stones and low fences, treading graves without discrimination. The truck gained the street. A taxi waited, half a block away, before a confectioner's.

With rare presence of mind, Tommy told the man to follow the dark truck, driving slowly as he passed the cemetery gate. Ray leaped to the running board and fell in the cab.

"Get up close enough to get that license number, quick. Then slow down and keep far enough back of them so they don't know we're following them."

"What'd they do, chief?"

"They been stealin' flowers off the graves."

"Yeah?"

"That's-right. Tommy, got a pencil? You got a pencil?"

"Sure," said the driver. "I need it back."

"Thanks."

Ray scribbled the license number on the back of an envelope.

"Now you want me to drop back?"

"No. Stay about this far away. They've turned their lights on now. Oh, boy! This is the life. What a film this will make!"

"You gonna put it in a picture?"

"*Am* I? Boy, and how!"

"You want me to pick up a cop?" asked the inquisitive chauffeur.

"Not on your life. We're from the bureau."

"O. K.!"

For five minutes, there was no incident. The two cars continued on half lighted thoroughfares, in traffic and out. Then the truck darted into a side street and sped quickly away at forty or forty-five.

"After 'em. For Pete's sake, don't let 'em get away."

"Say, Ray. They're gonna notice us following them."

Around another corner, the truck stopped before a dingy dwelling.

"Keep right on going, fellow. Don't stop. Go on to the corner."

"This is the bunk, Tommy. They're not gonna stop there. They're testing us out. Stop here."

As Ray paid the cab, he spoke rapidly to Tom. "Run across the street and go back slowly to the corner. Walk past the truck and wait at the next corner for me. Don't mind if they see you. They don't know you."

"*Maybe* they don't know me."

"If it's anybody that knows you, they'll be more scared than you."

Tommy did as he was bidden.

As he reached the corner, the three men left the driver's seat of the truck and walked away, one at a time, in different directions.

"If you want to go ahead with this," Ray told the cabby, "drive to the corner two blocks up the street that truck parked on, then come back down that street in the opposite direction."

"Much obliged, but my aunt is awful sick down on Fourteenth Street, an' I have to go home to give her 'er medicine."

"All right. So long."

The cab turned and fled for the more brilliantly lighted thoroughfare four blocks away.

One of the men from the truck, a tall, heavy fellow with a smooth, moon face passed Tommy with a suspicious glance, tarried for a moment at the corner, then turned in the direction taken by the departing taxi. The other two men had disappeared. Ray saw the man pause and silently prayed that Tommy had not betrayed himself. Reaching the corner, he followed Tommy on the opposite side of the street. The truck was deserted.

"Now, what'll I do? If the keys were in it, I could get in and drive it away. But they probably took the keys."

A swarthy giant in a dark overcoat stood in the shadow of a tree near the corner. Ray had not seen him until he was upon him. The best defense is offense. Shock for shock! "Have you got a match, friend?"

"Yeah."

Ray lit a cigarette and offered the pack to the man.

"T'anks."

"Thank you." He passed on. If only Tommy stayed away from him now! They must not be seen together. The fellow had started slowly in the opposite direction. Turning, Ray saw Tommy in a dark doorway, watching the tall man's departure. A hedge seemed to offer refuge. Ray turned in and stood waiting.

The ghoul followed his partner's course, turning toward the lighted street. There was still a third man to deal with. He was probably watching one or both of them now. A throttling arm slid from the darkness behind him and closed under his chin. Without attempting to turn, he kicked backward at the shin that must be supporting that arm. His assailant howled, and, in the fraction of a second the arm loosened, Ray had turned and sent his fist smashing to the other man's jaw.

After the first cry of pain, there was not another sound except for the scuffling of feet and the soft thuds of terrific blows.

The cry had brought Tommy on the run. He pounced on the fellow from behind, and the three rolled to the sidewalk in a tangled mass of squirming arms and legs. Between them, the two young fellows finally subdued the larger, older man. They bound him thoroughly, hands and feet with neckties and handkerchiefs. They gagged him with a piece torn from the tail of his own shirt, and rolled him under the hedge out of sight.

The fracas had not lasted more than three or four minutes. No one had passed. The honest householders of the vicinity had slept through it all.

"Say, we'd be in a nice mess if this guy wasn't on that truck," Tommy said when they had walked out of earshot.

"He was on it. You didn't hear him yelling, did you? If he wasn't afraid of the law, he'd have screamed blue murder. Now, listen, Tom. These babies have only parked here for a blind. They meant to scatter and watch. Then come back. This guy waiting proves it. The others have piked off toward the main hike. Now we're helpless without a cab. One will never pass here. One of us has to go get one."

"What are you gonna do with him?"

"Leave him here. He won't dare yell for help, and he's tied so he can't get away."

"Shall I run and get a cab?"

"Yes, and, for Pete's sake, hurry! This bird not coming back will hold them a little while."

"I'll hurry."

Ray returned to the prostrate form. "What's the idea of stealing that body, fellow? Who hired you?"

Black eyes glared defiance from the grass.

"If you'll tell me who is footing this bill, I'll let you go. Will you tell me?"

The man struggled vigorously to free his hands.

"You're not too well tied. I guess I better give you another rope or two for luck." He tore both sleeves from his shirt and shredded them, then twisted and braided the cloth into a sizable rope. He added this to the already secure shackles and stood up.

"Now listen. I'll come back here for you before dawn. Don't try to get away. You'll be shot. Just lie still and you'll be all right."

Tommy found a cab. He made a two-block circuit and came up the quiet street where the truck and Ray waited.

"Hold it here," Tommy instructed the driver. "We're waiting for that truck to move."

Ray watching down the street, saw the cab stop a block away. "The boy is all right. Once he gets out of this mess, he'll make a good undertaker."

The man who had given him the match had walked around several squares and returned; he passed close enough to touch Ray, but the hedge concealed both captor and captive.

From another direction came the fellow's companion. They debated on the corner, then crossed to their truck.

"Where's that bum gone to?"

"Maybe he got caught."

"Caught! He's lost his nerve. I knew he wouldn't stick. We'll wait just one minute, then we'll blow."

"You think everything is O. K.?"

"Nobody's been near the truck."

"There's a cab back there."

"It ain't the same one."

"No."

"Spooners."

"I wish I'd let this thing alone."

"Aw, shut up! You can blow now if you want to. I'd just as soon keep it all."

"I'll stick, but let's get out o' here."

"Aw right." The truck moved quickly away.

The cab started. Ray frantically cast about for a way to get their prisoner in the cab without arousing the driver's suspicion. Nothing seemed practical. "Tommy, you stay here. I'm sorry. I don't see any other way. I'll hurry back. If he starts to squawk, put your foot in his face."

Then to the driver, he said: "Follow that truck!"

2
· THE WHIZZING TRUCK

JACOBS called his office from a drug-store booth. "Hello, Saint—Jake."

"Yeah."

"Saint, Frisbee's got Evansborough under cover. He's sent him to some place in Maine until he wants him. It's a dirty trick. He's only done that to keep him away from us. He's scared he'll talk."

"Find out where he is an' go up there."

"I said Maine, not Scarsdale."

"Come on in! I want t' talk to you."

"All right."

He left the booth and started to cross the street when a truck whizzed past, just beating the changing traffic lights. A cab stopped directly in his path.

Ray opened the door. "Jake!"

"Hello, boy. How's the sleuth?"

"Get in here."

"What's up?"

"Did you see that little truck that just went by?"

"See it. It almost killed me."

"Jake, the biggest story you ever wrote is in that truck."

"Uh-huh! How come you're so friendly? I thought I was the last word in a rat."

"Well, I need you. I'm still sore, but I need you."

"I refuse to be used."

The lights changed.

"Catch him, boy. Listen, if you knew what was in that truck, you'd be glad you ran into me."

"Don't try to kid me along. What is in the truck."

"The body that Frisbee thinks he's going to find in Macnaughton's vault to-morrow."

The reporter leaned out toward the driver. "Faster, fellow. Never mind the law." He pulled his head back in and squinted at Ray. "Now, will you say that again?"

"The body that Frisbee intends to exhume tomorrow. The body they all think is Frank Daniels."

"In that truck?"

"Yes!"

"F' Heaven's sake! Whose truck?"

"I don't know. Tommy and I been trailin' 'em all night. They cracked the tomb and took coffin an' all. We watched 'em."

"What were you doin' there?"

"I went to get a look at that guy myself. I've got his wife all primed to identify him and everything. Tommy, too."

"You found the kid again?"

"Yes, you bum."

"Say, is this good? Who are these body snatchers?"

"I haven't any idea, but here's something else. Tommy is now standin' guard over one of the ghouls 'way up in the Bronx. We've got him tied and gagged under a bush on Whitcomb and

Cherry Street. God knows what's happened there since I left. Can you go see?"

"How'll I find you later? Y'mean let you go ahead after this truck?"

"Yes."

"Anybody else know about this?"

"Not a soul."

"My car's in the garage. I could go up an' get Tommy an' your prisoner."

"Take it to my house. I can't get in myself."

"Why not *my* house?"

"Yours is too easy to get out of. Even Tommy managed it."

"All right, your house. Then what?"

"Call your office. I'll leave a message there."

"Good! But, Ray, don't let anybody in on it. This has got to be exclusive."

"You think I'm crazy?"

"I've always been suspicious."

"Stop the car."

"So long."

"I'll call your office."

"Go ahead."

3
WHOLESALE CAPTURE

TOMMY's prisoner had given him no trouble at all. Their improvised shackles had held tightly. To avoid suspicion, the boy had sat on a basket well concealed from the street. For what seemed an interminable length of time, he sat waiting. He dared not smoke. He only breathed when it seemed absolutely necessary.

Finally, stiff from cold and his uncomfortable position, he walked gingerly to the corner and slowly back. The quiet was oppressive. He looked at the man on the ground. His position was unchanged. He walked again to the corner.

Jake's roadster was standing at the curb beside him before he was conscious of its approach. "Hello, Tommy."

"Hello." The boy was immediately suspicious.

"Where's your man. Ray said you had a fellow tied up. He sent me to get you."

"I ain't got nobody. You ain't even seen Ray."

"Yes, I have, Tommy. Oh, for Heaven's sake, don't get this muddled. Ray sent me to pick up you and this man. We're to take the guy to Ray's house and leave him and then go to Ray."

"Where is Ray?"

"He's still following that truck with the dead body in it."

"Oh, what'd he have to send you for? You'll steal the guy."

"No, I won't, Tommy. Honest, I'm with you. Ray and I are friends."

"You're a swell friend. Lockin' me up."

"That was my bull, Tommy. Honest, I'm on the square. Where's this guy?"

"He's here."

Together, they carried the man to the car, his eyes blaspheming at their every step.

As Jake shifted gears, he began to talk. "Can you drive this car?"

"Sure."

"Then you sit at the wheel while I phone the office. Ray is gonna call me there. Keep the motor running and watch for cops. If one comes near you, drive like the devil. Got me? We don't want this guy pinched until the last minute. We want the story complete when we do print it."

"I got you."

"Ray is going to call my office and leave word where we can find him. I'll run in a drug store and call. Don't leave unless you see something suspicious. Then, if you do leave, get in a quiet place and call my office yourself. Either Ray or I will leave a message there for you."

"What would I do with this guy?"

"I don't think you'll have to run. But if you do, take him to Ray's home."

"There's cops out in front, waiting for Ray and that crazy guy."

"Well, I don't think you'll have to go. But sit at the wheel, anyway. I'll stop here."

Jake had scarcely left the machine when a patrolman who might have been trying back doors to see if they were locked came from the end of the dark alley. Tommy took fright. There had been too much talk of "if". He stepped on the gas, braved the lighted street, and drove madly downtown.

He eased the roadster round Ray's corner and parked—fifty feet from the two detectives. He shut off the motor, took the keys from the magneto, and nonchalantly slammed the door. He walked around the corner, looked back at the two men, then ran to a cigar store a block away.

He called the *Record,* got the city desk, and asked for a message.

"Are you 'Tommy'?"

"Yes, sir."

"You're to go to the foot of Fleet Street to the dock. Your friend and Jake will be waiting for you. And you ain't to talk. Don't talk to anybody. Not even your own mother."

"No, sir."

"And listen. There's a 'package'—get that?—'a package' in the door pocket of Jake's car. You are to bring that along."

"A package?"

"Yes, a long, slim, shiny package that ain't wrapped up. Listen, son. This is New York State, and no one is allowed to have that kind of a package in his possession. Handle it carefully. Have you got it now?"

"Oh, yeah, I guess so."

Now he had to go back, within reach of those detectives and take—a gun?—from the pocket of the car.

Neither of the detectives heeded him. They were in animated conversation. The gagged prisoner only glared. In the door pocket was a .38 caliber revolver. As he transferred it to his pocket, the prisoner closed his eyes, consumed with futile rage.

Then Tommy jumped into a taxi and gave the address, forgetful, for the moment, that his pockets contained but thirty or forty cents.

"Now, what'll I do?"

When it did occur to him, he blushed, sickened and tried to efface himself against the cushions. What could he do? Ray was depending upon him. He had to get there quickly. Perhaps he could find him readily, and he would pay the bill. If Ray was not there—He fingered the revolver in his pocket with a growing assurance. He had heard of others holding up cabs. He could at least drive this one away—with the gun.

He rehearsed five different versions of that scene between Times and Union Squares. The traffic had lightened to a few desultory cabs. The lights were off for the night, and his chauffeur drove into the Bowery at better than forty. What if he should run into a cop at the docks? What if he were searched? He could never explain that gun. He was already wanted.

The driver spoke through the window. "That fellow want you?"

On the corner, Ray waved both arms.

"Yes."

The cab stopped.

Gosh, I'm glad you're here. I haven't got any money.

Ray laughed. "What a boy! I'll pay him. Watch that light down the street. If it goes out, tell me."

The taxi driver made change. "You fellows be goin' back uptown?"

"Why, yes. A little later. You want to wait?"

"It's about the only chance I'll get to haul out o' here to-night."

"All right. Turn around and wait over there. It may be some time."

"That's all right. I'll wait—an hour, anyway."

"It's still on," Tommy said.

"Did the door open?"

"No."

They walked in the gloomy street toward the water front.

"Those two fellows are in that shanty trying to get the watchman drunk. They left the coffin in the car and drove it into that stone shed.

"My idea is they want to put the body on that barge that's loading, but they don't want the watchman in on it."

"Are they sailors?"

"I think so. They aren't sure about this old fellow in the shanty. They're feeding him gin by the glassful. Where did you leave Jake?"

"Way uptown. He went to call his office, and a cop came along, so I drove away."

"Where's the other guy?"

"In front of your house in Jake's car."

"Out in front?"

"Yes. I didn't know what to do with him."

"My God! I wonder if he'll talk."

"He won't talk until they take that rag out of his mouth."

"Sh-sh!"

"They're coming out."

The door of the little shanty opened, and the two grave robbers emerged, carefully closing the door behind them. Tommy and Ray hugged the wall. The men crossed the road quietly and entered the wide door of a stone shed.

"I got Jake's gun."

"You have?"

"Yes."

"Gimme."

Inside the shed, a flash light played on the rear of the truck.

Come on, Tommy, pretend you've got a gun, too, but if they start to shoot, fall down." Together they crossed to the shed.

"Stick 'em up, you fellows, and keep that flash light high!"

The beam of light swung only as far as the leveled revolver. When its shining barrel was revealed, four hands stretched skyward.

"Get the light, Tommy! Stay to one side so I won't plug you."

Tommy took the light from the brawny hand of the ghoul.

"Now keep that light on them while I go through 'em."

Tommy pointed the torch at the frightened men.

"What's the idea?" asked one of them half-heartedly. "You hijackers won't find nothin' here."

"No? Well, boy, you're going to find something in the morning."

Ray took a revolver from each of the men. "Now go look the car over, Tom. See if there's anything in it to shoot with, first. Then open the hood, take out the spark plugs and bust the magneto. I'll just keep these boys here. Keep your hands high!"

"If you fellows want to tell me who hired you to do this job, I'll see if I can't get you off. How about it?"

"We ain't done nothin'. What you talkin' about?"

"All right, have it your own way. All set, Tom?"

"Yeah. Here's another gun."

"See if all those guns are loaded."

Tommy broke the revolvers and inspected the chambers. "They're full."

"Fine. Just leave 'em on the floor. Hand me one of 'em."

"You gonna open the coffin now, Ray?"

"It's better to let it stay sealed since it's been stolen. See? No. I think we'll tie these boys up and lock them in here. Then go get the cops."

"Now listen, fellow. If you want to know who hired us, I'll tell you. What do we get out of it? Will you let us go?"

"I'd do what I could for you."

"Would you let us go?"

"Nope. Your pal has already squealed. We got him hours ago."

"Yeah!"

"We got him while you were parked in the Bronx."

"And he squealed?"

"He spilled everything."

"The bum!"

"That won't get you anywhere. He squealed to save his hide. If you know what's good for you, you'll do the same. Tommy, see if that's Jake coming."

Tommy peered out of the door. "He's on the corner paying a cab."

"Good. Now, just to see if this other bird was giving us a bum steer—who hired you?"

"Mr. Carr hired us—the lawyer."

"Go get Jake, Tommy. Give me the light."

Tommy ran to the street and returned with the reporter.

"Listen, Ray, here's another hot one," Jake blurted. "I called your house, and the landlady says Sybil just phoned from Trenton that she's in Daniels' house with Richard Roe."

"Yeah? And what?"

"She wants you to come over there."

"What'll I do with these birds?"

"Turn 'em over to the law."

"And give your story away?"

"How can we help it? It looks like Roe is Daniels."

"I've known that for a month."

"But it's the biggest story! "

"Bigger than this grave robbery?"

"Well, just as big."

"But why can't we have both?"

"How?"

"We'll tie these babies up and leave Tommy to guard 'em. Then you and I'll go to Trenton."

"It'll take hours."

"Not so long. We'll take your car."

"But it's getting daylight."

"What of it? We'll lock these fellows in here. Give Tom a gun and set him at the door. If they make a peep or if anybody comes for the truck, all Tommy has to do is call a cop."

"That sounds all right. But the cops must have found their partner. What if he talks?"

"He's too scared to talk."

One of the two huskies found his voice. "You fellows'll pay for this. I'll get you if it takes a lifetime."

"Shut up or you'll sleep in a cell."

"It looks like a cell to me if I shut up or not."

"That's no stage joke. Tommy, is that wire there on the floor?"

"Yeah, wire."

"Good! Make these boys some handcuffs."

"Oh, you will, will you?"

"Shut up! I'll crown you!"

With coils of thin copper wire, found in a tangle on the floor, both men were securely trussed, ankles and wrists, then stretched beside the coffin in their truck.

"Now we'll shut this and lock it." A padlock, still containing the key, hung from the staple in the door jamb.

"Tommy, you're stuck again. Here's a gun, but don't use it. Keep it in your pocket just to scare these boys with. But don't use it. Stay close by until you hear from us, and, in case of trouble, call a cop. Don't forget. If they try to get away, make 'em get back. If anybody comes with a key to that lock, get a policeman. We'll come for you or send for you just as soon as we can."

"All right, Ray. I'll stay here. Here's your keys, Jake. Your car's in front of Ray's."

"So long."

"So long."

CHAPTER TWENTY-TWO

1
SYBIL GRIEVES

P HILLIPS was aroused from his midnight sleep by the racing of a motor under the window. He stuck his gray head out and saw his supposedly dead employer hand a lady out of the car. He withdrew his puzzled, sleep-filled head and, swathed in a dressing gown, descended to open the door.

Richard Roe looked at him blankly.

"Hello."

How do you do, Mr. Daniels? How do you do? I'm glad to see you, sir. Glad to see you alive and well."

Sybil clutched Richard Roe's arm. Mr. Daniels! Richard Roe was Mr. Daniels? Then he was married! Then—she—he—it could never be. The largeness of the moment was lost upon her. Hers was a personal loss. The State of New York and its murders were nothing. The Atlantic Insurance Company with its charges was nothing. She had lost a lover. Richard Roe was gone. In his stead, there remained a married man—who had lost his mind.

"What's that?" Richard Roe inquired. "Daniels? Say, I know you, don't I?"

"You should, sir. I'm Phillips. I've worked for you a long time."

"You work for me?"

"Yes, sir."

"What did you say my name was?"

"Your name is Daniels, sir. Surely, you know that."

"Is that right, Sybil? Is my name Daniels?"

Sybil grasped a straw. "Your name is Richard Roe."

"Sure. This guy's crazy. I'm Richard Roe. You're mistaken. I'm not Daniels."

"But what are you doing here, then? Surely, sir, you are Mr. Daniels. This is his home. That is his car you are driving."

"Is that so?"

"Certainly."

"Sybil, do you think there's anything in that? That's my car, all right. I've driven that car many a mile."

"And isn't this your house, sir?"

"Well, it—I thought it was. It—it looks familiar. Say, now. I've heard that name before. Oh, Sybil! Say, they—they said I killed Frank Daniels. The—the police said I killed Frank Daniels."

"You'd have to commit suicide to do that, sir."

"That's what they said."

"I'm going to call your uncle, Mr. Daniels. He'll recognize you."

"My uncle, eh?"

"Yes, sir. Tell me, do you remember him?"

"No. I don't. Come on, Sybil, sit down. I—I'll have to look around here, I guess. Who did you say you were?"

"I'm John Phillips. I work in your hardware store."

"Have I got a hardware store?"

"Why, certainly. You must remember the store."

"I don't remember anything."

"Excuse me, please. I must telephone."

The old man roused Robert Daniels.

"Your nephew is here, sir, with a woman. He doesn't seem to know me nor remember you. But he has his car—and this strange woman."

"I'll be right over."

2
THE STORY BREAKS

TIRED, bedraggled and dirty, Ray and Jacobs stumped, stiff-legged from the roadster to the Daniels door. Ray rang the bell. Old man Phillips opened the door.

"Is Sybil here? Sybil or Richard Roe. We received a call——"

The girl recognized Ray's voice.

"Oh, Mr. Fitzgerald!" Tears stained her cheeks. "Richard Roe is Frank Daniels, and this man works for him, and this is his darling uncle. Mr. Daniels, this is Mr. Fitzgerald. He knows all about everything."

"That's a pretty large order, Sybil. I'm glad to know you, Mr. Daniels."

"Sybil has been telling us that you were solving this murder."

"I've been working on it. In fact, I was pretty sure that our Richard Roe was Mr. Daniels."

"Well, it's a wonder you haven't said so."

"There were more angles to the case than you imagine. You see, there *was* a murder that night, even if your nephew was not killed."

"Is that so?"

"Yes, sir. And I have been piecing the whole thing together. It has taken some time."

"I can imagine."

"Is Mr. Daniels aware of his identity now?"

"He is in bed up stairs with two of the best doctors in Trenton. They say that, when he awakes, he will know who he is and will be able to tell me everything that happened to him."

"But," Sybil added, "he won't remember anything that happened to him while he was Richard Roe. He—he won't remember you—or me."

"That's too bad, Sybil. But you must realize he is a married man."

"I know it." The tears came in a flood. "That's just it!"

"Can I use the phone?" Jake asked.

"Certainly. It's in the hall."

"City desk. Put Lester on, this is Jake. Hello, Les? Get this, Les, and stand by for more. Richard Roe has been identified as Frank Daniels. He is now in his own home recovering from brain storm. All credit to the *Record*. This is exclusive. And more! Hold it! Frisbee is going to exhume a body in Glenn View early to-day. That body will be missing. It was stolen last night. The *Record* will publish the full account of the grave robbery told by an eyewitness. The *Record* will also produce the body late this afternoon."

"What?" The wires hummed under the impact of that electrically reproduced bellow.

"Yes, you dumb-bellow. I've got it in my pocket."

"Jake, you're nuts."

"I've got the body and the men who stole it. By the way, see if you can get Mike over to the offices of the Atlantic Insurance Company to interview Carr, the lawyer. That will be a nice side light on the story when I get back."

"I'll get this in the bulldog, Jake. But it's our hides if there's anything phony about it."

"There's nothin' phony about it. Razz the police. Call 'em children. Tell them the *Record* will produce the missing coffin this afternoon."

"Where is it now?"

"None o' your business. Write what I tell you. You can have the story on the street by the time the body is missing."

"Jesus, it's a bear. We've got the empty tomb. Everybody's got that. But this is——"

"More! In the final edition to-night, the *Record* will carry the complete and authentic account of exactly what happened on October third and fourth, with signed and sworn testimony and photographs of every one concerned. And that's exclusive, too. We can't even tell it to the district attorney by that time, but you can have it in print. I'm writing it now. Play it up in every edition. It'll be complete in the final."

CHAPTER TWENTY-THREE

1
THE STORY IN FULL

R AY and Assistant District Attorney Frisbee were alone with two court stenographers in the latter's office.

"I will begin with the actions of Mr. Frank Daniels on October third, and I will trace every move of every principal in this case up to the present. I will make many charges as I tell my story and you will, of course, proceed as you see fit in each case. I have, for proof, the confessions and testimony of a dozen people. I will guess very little."

"Go on, Mr. Fitzgerald. The least of your crimes so far has not been modesty."

"Daniels left his home at nine thirty in the morning. He went to his hardware store and took ten dollars from the cash register. He wore a brown suit—the suit your assistants sent to his uncle, Robert Daniels, for identification. He carried several letters and cards which would identify him, and a gold hunting-case watch.

"He took a noon train to New York, and, upon his arrival, went immediately to the office of Samuel Epstein on Broadway where he collected a debt of more than seven hundred and fifty dollars.

"He ate a lunch near Epstein's office, then took a subway train to Times Square. He walked from there to the undertaking parlor of Joseph Chandler to pay a visit to his friend and his wife's friend, Mr. Charles Everett.

"I have all these details from Mr. Daniels himself. None of it is conjecture.

"He talked to Mr. Everett only a few minutes, invited him to call, asked where the wash room was and was told it was out of order. You can easily verify that assertion. I have learned from Tommy Freeman that that was true.

"He crossed the street on leaving Everett, entered the Bond Building and rode to the fourth floor. It was not the first time he had used this wash room. On other visits to New York when he had not wished to bother Mr. Everett, he had used this lavatory. It was an extraordinary place, in this sense: it had no lettering on the door, was in fact, used very little. Some of the tenants of the building did not know what the little room contained.

"When he entered it, another man was there, washing his hands. He dried them on a paper towel and turned quickly upon Mr. Daniels, who saw a blow coming too late to dodge. This man struck Mr. Daniels with a short piece of iron pipe which I have here."

Ray placed a cylindrical package in white paper on Frisbee's desk.

"Instead of hitting his head, as he may have intended to, he hit his neck. The back of Mr. Daniels' head and neck now reveal three contusions, only one of which broke the skin. You will be able to get expert testimony if you want it from the two Trenton doctors now attending him.

"These blows immediately rendered Mr. Daniels unconscious. He dropped to the floor. The man whose photographs I now hand you was a former employee of the firm of manufacturing jewelers whose offices are next to this wash room in the

Bond Building. His name was Sigmund Ladensky and he lived on Plymouth Avenue with his wife. There were no children.

"Mr. Daniels has identified these photographs as pictures of his assailant.

"There was a bolt on the inside of this washroom door—and now I am guessing for a few minutes. Ladensky pushed that bolt and stayed inside with Frank Daniels, taking more than seven hundred and fifty dollars and his gold watch from the body. He stayed within until he thought the floor was deserted for the night, intending to enter the offices of his former employer and rob him of gold and precious stones.

"Ladensky had been a trusted employee. He knew the combinations of the safes and vaults. He had keys to the doors. He had lost his job for inciting the other workmen in the place to strike for higher wages. He was known to bear a grudge. He had been heard to threaten to 'get even' with Mr. Bloom, president of the company. The day before, that is, October second, Mr. Bloom had had every combination changed, in fear of that very visit. The locks were to be changed also so that Ladensky's keys would be useless, but, on October third, this had not been done. Nor had the burglar alarm been altered.

"Mr. Bloom found his burglar alarm spiked the next morning, indicating that Ladensky had been there but had been unable to open any of the vaults containing valuables, since nothing was missing.

"On October third, Ladensky wore a very old gray suit. He stood on the window ledge of the little wash room and put this piece of pipe on a corner of the sprinkler-system piping where it remained unnoticed until I found it.

"It bears finger prints which will tally with those of Ladensky as I will later show. He must have worked in the jeweler's for some time, probably two hours or more attempting to open the safes, because this is what happened before he left the building.

"Frank Daniels partially regained consciousness. He dragged himself to the fire exit of the building and down the four flights of steps to the street where he collapsed, partially paralyzed.

"In the meantime, Charles Everett had met Mrs. Daniels and they had bought tickets to Chicago, checked their baggage and retired to the Blackstone Hotel for the night, registered as Mr. and Mrs. Charles Everett. You will find that name in Everett's hand on the register of that date.

"A simpering bell boy, more than forty years old, is ready to testify that the couple did not leave the room after eight o'clock; that they had dinner in their room. His memory is prompted by a large tip and a naturally filthy mind. He has a vivid imagination and an unlimited resource for remembering details suggestive of lewdness.

"It is impossible to connect either of them with the assault upon the person of Frank Daniels.

"The two men who found Daniels' supposedly dead body shortly after nine o'clock are John Peterson and Francis Kelly, both employed by the Klabe Hat Store on Forty-fifth Street. They left the store at nine o'clock and proceeded west toward Broadway. Peterson stepped in the Bond Building hallway to light a cigarette and stumbled upon the body.

"These two men are ready to identify Mr. Frank Daniels, the man the police have been calling Richard Roe, as the man they carried to the rear of Chandler's undertaking parlor and stretched on a table with the help of Tommy Freeman. Both of these men thought Daniels was dead, being unable to feel any breath or to hear or detect any motion of the heart. There was a general stiffness on his left side which these two men assumed was the natural stiffness of a dead man.

"Tommy Freeman, the only person in the undertaking parlor, is only a boy. He was left in charge of the place that night for the first time in his life. He was going to embalm his first body unaided. He was alone with eight thousand dollars of his employer's money. He wondered if he could open the safe. He had watched Everett do it repeatedly. He had memorized the combination."

"What for?" Frisbee interrupted quickly.

"I don't believe he knows. I think it was a normal curiosity. Just a boy's natural greed for facts. I was like that. Don't you think it was natural?"

"No. I think he meant to open it some night and walk away with the cash. Tell me, where is this Tommy now?"

"He is with the police who are bringing your missing body to you."

"You mean the body that was stolen last night?"

"That's the one."

"Well, go on with your story. You've got a lot to tell yet."

"Well, Tommy had been fooling with the safe. He wanted to see if he could open it. He wanted to see that eight thousand dollars."

"Wanted to *see* it. That's good!" Frisbee guffawed with heavy meaning.

Ray stuck tenaciously to his story. He dared not allow the man's ridicule to undermine Tommy's character.

"He had never seen so much money at one time before. It was a novelty to him. He was in charge of that money. He was guarding it. But locked in the safe, it would have been safe enough if he were not there. He wanted to feel that it was up to him to keep that money; he wanted the thrill of being personally responsible for its safety."

"We'll waive all that, Mr. Fitzgerald. Did he open the safe?"

"Yes. He couldn't do it at first. The combination eluded him. But he had just succeeded when these two men arrived, carrying Frank Daniels. He had just opened the door.

"As any officer who ever had that beat at night will testify, you cannot see that safe readily from the street. There is but one angle that affords a view of it. The men who stood at the door could not see the boy.

"He answered their summons and took in the body. The men left and reported their find to the patrolman at the corner. He came to the parlor, talked to Freeman for a moment and went away, calling the morgue from his box on the corner.

"Tommy was upset. He didn't know what to do. He undressed the body, scarcely aware of his own actions. Then he remembered the money, and the open safe door. He went to get the money, and, as he held it in his hand, some one grabbed him from the back.

"That also was Ladensky. The boy has identified those photographs as pictures of his assailant.

"It is my theory that, after being unable to make any headway, in the jeweler's, Ladensky left the Bond Building, crossed the street, and quite by accident saw the boy with this large bundle of bills in his hand, stooping beside the safe.

"He entered the undertaking parlor and grabbed Tom. The boy broke away from him and ran to the back of the shop, throwing the bundle of bills into a dark corner of the hall as he ran. He eluded the big man and returned to the front of the parlor. The fellow followed him, threateningly, and Tom seized a heavy chair and swung it against the fellow's head.

"That body, with its neck and jaw broken by that chair, will be found in the Macnaughton coffin when you open it."

"You're sure of that, are you?"

"Positive. The man fell dead. Tommy became panic-stricken. He looked for the money, but could not find it. He ran around the parlor like a mad person. He was frightened sick. He had allowed strangers to bring in an unidentified body. He was afraid that was wrong. He had undressed it. He was afraid that was wrong. He had lost the money. He knew darn well that was wrong. And now he had killed a man. He didn't know what to do. Finally, he dragged the body into the back room and stuffed it far back under a table. Then he ran."

"The boy told you all this himself, didn't he?"

"Yes, sir."

"Go on."

"The door had a spring lock which could be opened from the inside but not the outside. Frank Daniels came to. He was groggy from the blows he had received. He got off the table and wandered into the front of the parlor. He looked around for something to put on. In a clothes press, he found Tommy's raincoat.

"That coat is in this package. Sybil Neipling, the maid in my house, will testify that she found Frank Daniels, clad in that raincoat, near the corner of Forty-fifth Street and Sixth Avenue, shortly after ten o'clock that evening. Tommy Freeman will identify the garment as his. His mother will corroborate his testimony.

"Since Daniels' memory was worthless, this, too, is conjecture. But the facts indicate that, clad in the raincoat, Daniels left the undertaking parlor, without closing the door tightly and wandered to the corner without meeting any one until he passed Sybil who took him in tow."

"Why didn't she report him to the police at once? Why didn't you?"

"She didn't report him because she had no sweetheart, and he seemed simple enough to like her. She felt as if she had found something priceless. Finders are keepers, you know. And I didn't report it because I didn't care, in the first place, and, in the second place, I felt sorry for the girl and was glad enough to let her have her man unmolested.

"The ambulance came to Chandler's, and the men picked up the body of Clark C. Macnaughton and the clothing of Frank Daniels. The incompetent medical examiner handed in a report that would discredit a freshman in medical school. He looked at a body that had been killed in an auto accident twenty-four hours before and reported that the man had been killed with a dull hatchet that evening."

"He has been removed. That report was inexcusable."

"The next morning, Joseph Chandler arrived in his undertaking parlor. He went in, expecting to find everything in readiness for a big funeral. Instead, he could not even find a body. He immediately telephoned his general manager, thinking that for some reason the Macnaughton funeral was to be held from one of the other branches. He was assured that the funeral was to be from No. 4, and that the body was there. He took no one into his confidence, fearing consequences, but he made a hurried tour of all of the parlors, inspecting them all. Then, finding no body in any of them, he returned to No. 4. How he came upon the body of Ladensky under the table, I do not know. He has never given me any help. But you will easily be able to verify these telephone calls and his nervous visits to the other parlors because every employee was impressed with the disappearance of Everett and Tommy, and they all recall young Chandler's agitation.

"I have made no attempt to prove anything against Mr. Chandler. I have sought only to explain his actions that day. If there is any reason for prosecuting him, I believe you will find it easy to prove that he embalmed Ladensky himself. Since he is not much of an undertaker, in fact, knows very little about his business, there will doubtless be many marks of the novice on Ladensky's body. Tommy Freeman laughs at Chandler's attempts to attend a dead body.

"This is my theory, at any rate. You can imagine Chandler's state of mind. One does not mislay dead bodies. If one does, one tries to keep it a secret. After all, it wasn't a thing that could be noised about. No one would intrust their dead to an undertaker who was liable to replace the remains."

"He should have reported the disappearance to the police at once," Frisbee said testily.

"He should have, Mr. Frisbee, but he didn't want to ruin the reputation his father had worked so hard to build. He found a body that would do. He only had a few minutes, an hour at most, after he had gone to all his other parlors.

"He put Ladensky on the table and embalmed him. Calling in the police would have delayed one of the biggest funerals of the year, and he knew that the casket would not be opened. You can get plenty of testimony to bear out my theory. Every one has noticed his nervous behavior.

"That evening he took the clothing of the unidentified man, wrapped it in a bundle and drove into Connecticut. He threw it away and returned to New York. A boy found it. It contained the stolen money collected by Daniels from Epstein and Frank Daniels' watch. I have identified that suit of clothes. Mrs. Ladensky recognized a piece of the goods the moment I showed it to her. The tailors who made the suit will testify that they sold it to him.

"When your Richard Roe, bothered by his subconscious or some equally hard-to-understand quirk of his alleged brain, went back and stood before his own store in Trenton, his clerk, Phillips, recognized him. The insurance company became suspicious and had Mrs. Daniels arrested in Chicago.

"An overly ambitious young attorney went too far. He made a great many more charges than he could prove. He was in very, very deep. There was almost nothing he would not do to get out. He even resorted to robbing a grave."

"You're quite a detective, young man. And I suppose you can produce him, too."

"Yes, sir. He is sitting in his own office this minute—with handcuffs on. They are unofficial handcuffs. They could get their owner in trouble. But we didn't want to risk losing him. So we took chances. My friend Jacobs of the *Record* got in to see him an hour ago, started to interview him, and got the bracelets on his wrists. He's waiting for a call from me."

"Thanks. We'll have to prosecute him."

"And Chandler?"

"I'll have to investigate that further—after I've seen what is in this coffin."

"Yes, sir. I may as well confess, Mr. Frisbee, that I just helped Chandler get away from your detectives. He's driven to Long Island to get married."

"You'd be better off if you'd mind your own business."

"There's only one thing I want to know."

"Yes? There are several I still want to know."

"I want to know who it was that crowned me on Forty-fifth Street the other night—not ten feet from where Daniels was first found."

"You didn't mention that before."

"No, I couldn't fit it into the pattern. Who could that have been? I've accounted for everything in the entire case but that."

"You may have satisfied yourself, young man, but you haven't satisfied me. In the first place, what became of Chandler's eight thousand dollars? And, in the second place, why did Tommy kill this so-called Ladensky and run? I'll have to hear the answers to those two questions before this case is ended."

2
"GOOD-BY!"

THE aged uncle of Frank Daniels grinned slyly at his nephew from the door. "You'll be up in a day or two. Up and around at your old tricks again, losing two dollars where only one was lost before. Good day."

"Good-by, Uncle Bob. Come again."

"Good-by."

"That," said Mrs. Daniels as the door closed, "is the most astonishing thing that has happened. Uncle Robert was never like that before."

Frank Daniels shook his head.

Everett raised his brows in polite surprise.

Sybil adjusted the counterpane carefully.

"Well, we'll be going, too, Frank."

"You're in wonderful hands," said Beatrice.

"Sybil's mighty good to me."

"She loves you, Frank."

Sybil blushed.

"Well," Richard Roe welled, "well, well——"

"And now that it's all over, we can get a decree in a month."

Everett cleared his throat.

"As soon as that?" the sick man asked.

"Yes. It doesn't take long. I have a good lawyer. Well, get better fast."

"I will, Bea. Sure I will, and you take good care of her, Charley. She's a fine woman."

"I know it, Frank."

"Well, good-by."

"Good-by."

"Good-by, Sybil."

"Good-by, Mrs.—Daniels."

"Good-by."

"Good-by."

The door closed.

After a long pause, Daniels cleared his throat. "Well, now that they're all gone—ain't you—gonna—kiss me, Sybil?"

3
WHERE THE MONEY WAS

THEY had thrown Ray out after the fourth or fifth interruption. They were concentrating on Tommy. Brubacher was there, and Frisbee and a tall fellow who had a reputation for getting confessions.

"Now, Tommy, your story don't hold water. You stole that money, an' you've got most of it right now. Where is it?"

"I threw it in the hall."

"If you threw it in the hall, why wasn't it found?"

"I don't know."

"This poor fellow Ladensky tried to stop you from stealing the money, and you killed him."

"I guess I killed him all right. I hit him as hard as I could with a chair. But I didn't steal the money. He was after it."

Roy paced the floor of the outer corridor.

"For heaven's sake, go sit down somewhere!" a deputy ordered gruffly. "That zoo stuff drives me nuts."

Ray tried to be genial. "They're trying to hang something on that kid, friend. And he didn't do a thing."

"Well, take it easy. Sit down! You ain't no tiger."

The elevator ejected Joseph Chandler and his bride, and Mrs. Clark C. Macnaughton, with her lawyer, who talked rapidly to Blanchard.

Chandler saw Ray. "Hello, young fellow. What's the matter? You look worried."

"I am worried, Mr. Chandler. They've got Tommy in there trying to make him confess that he stole your money and killed Ladensky to get away."

"But they can't do that."

"They threw me out."

"Well, we'll see if we can't fix that up. You wait here. I'll send out for you."

The group entered Frisbee's office.

On its next trip, the elevator discharged a man of medium height with a short-cropped brown mustache. He carried a traveling bag. Ray started toward him, wide-eyed in recognition, then stopped and watched him disappear through the same door.

"Who was that?" he asked the deputy.

"I don't know. Never saw him before."

"Well, I have!" Ray followed the man into the lion's den, regardless of consequences.

"I told you to stay out of here, Mr. Fitzgerald. We'll have to tell the police——"

"Mr. Frisbee, who is that man?"

"That is Doctor Evansborough."

"The medical examiner?"

"He *was*."

"The one that went over Mr. Macnaughton's body?"

"Yes."

"Well, he's the guy that crowned me on Forty-fifth Street that night."

"Is that so?"

"I'll say it's so." Turning to the doctor, he said: "No wonder you wanted me to drop the case."

"Why, I never saw you before in my life."

"No, well you'll see me again. I——"

"If you stay here, you'll have to be more quiet, Mr. Fitzgerald. We are conducting an inquiry."

"Mr. Frisbee, may I say a few words?" asked the widow of the famous lawyer.

"Certainly, Mrs. Macnaughton."

"It is just this. Every detail of this affair is so painful. I have suffered; Mr. Chandler has suffered. A great many people have been put to inconvenience, bother and pain. I do not know whether my wishes are of any moment or not, but, since your mystery has all been explained and you have found that no one but a poor lady, Mrs. Ladensky, has been harmed, can't the case be dropped? I will personally see that Mrs. Ladensky never wants for a thing as long as she lives. Surely, you have no cause to prosecute Mr. Chandler. He is an old friend of mine. I bear him no ill will for his part in the affair. What can be gained by continuing this case and keeping our names in the daily papers?"

"Well, Mrs. Macnaughton, I would like to do as you say. There is only one more point to be cleared up. I am sure that, if you are generous enough to care for Mrs. Ladensky, she will not wish to push the case. I have learned that she lived in dread of her late husband's brutality. His reputation was pretty bad.

"Mr. Chandler has committed a rather serious offense, but I think the State can afford to overlook it in view of the fact that we have apprehended the man's murderer."

"Who is that? Tommy?" Chandler asked.

"Yes, Mr. Chandler. I am not convinced that this boy struck in defense of property he was set to guard. In fact, I am almost certain that he still has your eight thousand dollars; buried somewhere, perhaps."

Brubacher could not resist the temptation. "Yes. The eight thousand dollars that you found."

"But, gentlemen, I *did* find it. I found it at the end of that dark hall between the parlor and the back room. I found it the night after the funeral."

"At the end of the hall?"

"Right where I threw it," Tommy cried.

"You can check with my bank. Besides the daily deposit made by my treasurer, you will find a deposit on that day, made by me in person, of eight thousand dollars. That amount was in a single packet of bills, bound with a rubber band, on the floor at the end of the hall."

"Well, I'll be————" started Brubacher.

Ray threw his arm around Tommy's shoulder. "There's your release, Tommy. I told you it would be all right."

Frisbee cleared his throat. "Well, I don't know. I'll have to talk it over with the district attorney. You can all go now. I—I don't see where there's any evidence against any one, at this time."

4
CASE DISMISSED

THAT night the *Record* printed the headline:

DANIELS-LADENSKY CASE DISMISSED
ATTORNEY FRISBEE WILL NOT
ASK FOR INDICTMENTS

The Daniels-Macnaughton-Ladensky mystery, which was solved by the efforts of a *Record* representative, drew to a close to-day when——

THE END.